I0763272

WELCOME TO PARADISE

Two Lonely People Searching for Paradise

Jim Hess

The characters in this book are purely fictional. The incidents and dialogue are not to be constructed as real. Any resemblance to actual events or persons, living or dead, is entirely coincidental.

ISBN: 978-1-7347481-2-3

Revised Edition 2024
Published April 2024 by
The Old Paths Publications, Inc
Email TOP@theoldpathspublications.com
www.theoldpathspublications.com

ABSTRACT

Two lonely people have a chance encounter which leads them to love and adventure in the Middle East. In their quest to find happiness they face peril and adventure that threatens their lives in Petra and Israel. They face terrorists and Bedouin tribes that transport them to another world.

THE AUTHOR

Jim Hess is a licensed marital and family therapist. He has traveled extensively to many places in the world as a minister and consultant. Jim also works with military bases in the United States and locations overseas. He may be reached at:

hessjim703@gmail.com

Photo of the author by David DePiazza.

TABLE OF CONTENTS

ACKNOWLEDGMENTS

To my children & grandchildren who are the inspiration for my work and travels.

CHAPTER 1 – JOHN

John was not sure where he was, so many faces in so many places. He'd had this feeling before. As he sat in a restaurant or a café, he often found himself trying to figure out just what city he was in.

Finally, he remembered he was in Bruges, Belgium. The sun was setting as he finished his main course at the small sidewalk café in the beautiful, ancient city. Handsome Patrician houses, impressive churches, and exquisite works of art are quiet testimonials to its glorious history. The canal flowing through the center of the city reflects the image of old buildings, churches, and homes. Boats float gently filled with wide-eyed tourists, their cameras clicking. The old town center comes alive each day as residents hurry to the shops. Housewives scurry about on their bicycles to purchase fresh bread, vegetables, and meat for evening meals as tourists gaze at the sidewalk artists, vendors, and other activities taking place in the open city square.

What a romantic scene, John thinks as he sits in the quaint little café eating dessert. He can't remember being in a town that has so much character or such wonderful tasting desserts. The aromas from a variety of exotic foods being prepared in the kitchen reach John. John glances at his watch and realizes that it is already dark at home in Denver, Colorado.

During the summer, the sun does not set until almost 10:00 pm in this part of the world. In his work as a management consultant, John travels to many parts of the world working for companies that manufacture military equipment.

John finished his meal and walked a few blocks to his hotel. He tried to think of something to do to fill the empty evening hours. This has always been the toughest part of the day when working on the road - lonely hotel rooms, often watching TV in languages that he doesn't understand. And as European TV is quite different from American TV stations because it is more sexually explicit, John, being a Christian, had to be extra careful to avoid pornography.

John decided to go for a walk. As he strolled along ancient stone sidewalks, he admired the beauty of this fifteenth century city. When he walked past the Pralinique, famous for its mouth-watering chocolate, he was enticed by the sweet smell of candies and pastries filling the air when a woman rushing out of the shop bumped into him.

"I am so sorry," she said. "I didn't see you."

"That is OK. I wasn't watching where I was going either." John was breathless; startled by the beauty of the woman. He was speechless as she disappeared around the corner. He stood for a moment still dazed by the beautiful green eyes of the graceful lady who had bumped into him and quickly walked away.

As John headed back to his hotel room, he recalled her features in his mind. He couldn't stop thinking about her – long blonde hair and thin figure with beautiful shapely legs, much like a model. He began to feel disappointed that he had no way to find out who she was or where she lived. From their brief encounter, he had detected a European accent.

He said his prayers and went to bed, tossing and turning for a time before finally falling asleep. His alarm woke him at 6 am the next morning. As he struggled to get out of bed, he stretched trying to wake himself up. He made coffee and picked up the paper lying outside of his room. After taking a shower, he headed down to the hotel restaurant for breakfast and then caught a cab to the client's offices to work.

Some client issues were easy enough to solve; others were more difficult. This client's situation fell into the difficult to impossible category. After several weeks of working on workflow redesigns, interpersonal issues, and human resource problems, John was anxious to go home – to the Rocky Mountains. He could hardly wait until the end of the week when he would catch a flight and go home to rest for a few days.

When John picked up the morning newspaper, he thumbed through it, looking at the pictures and trying to understand some of the stories. As he looked at pictures in the local news section, he froze. There in the picture was the green-eyed beauty who had run into him coming out of the sweet shop. He stuffed the page into his briefcase and headed to work.

Luckily, the plant manager John was working for is an American, so communication was not an issue. Most of the other team members were from various parts of Europe. There were obvious cultural differences, communication issues, and generational differences that were hindering their ability to work as a high-performing team. John had often admitted that people having trouble communicating kept him busy with work.

After a long day, John headed back to the hotel on foot. After fifteen years of being a consultant and being on the road so much, there was little glamor left for him in traveling. As he walked along, he thought about his life – there had been so many things he had wanted to accomplish when he was young that had fallen by the wayside. He had gotten so busy making money that he had not taken time to live. He remembered the words of a friend from his youth who told him "**when you learn enough to really live, you are old enough to die**." The longer I live the more I see the truth in those words, he thought.

Traveling had resulted in too many nights in lonely hotels, countless hours in airports waiting for flights, many flights on noisy, uncomfortable airplanes, and many rental cars, taxis, and trains. There had been too many deadlines and countless stressful meetings with dysfunctional companies. Life was passing him by.

He had planned to get married someday, have a family, and shuffle children around to soccer and baseball games. He had always wanted a daughter who would become a daddy's girl.

As he turned the corner to the hotel, he sighed. Well maybe it's not too late; perhaps things could be different. As he rode the elevator, he thought about his greatest desire of all – having the time to work on developing his spiritual life. He had always been a believer but in the hustle and bustle of life, he had lost his spiritual focus.

John went to his room and unloaded his briefcase. He stuck the page from the morning paper under his arm and headed out to look for a restaurant. The HR manager at the plant had recommended a nice seafood restaurant to John.

As he walked along in a crowded section of Bruges, he noticed two young men who seemed to be following him. After years of traveling in foreign countries, John had learned to be aware of his surroundings. Pickpockets and thieves are rampant in foreign countries. One pickpocket appearing on a recent BBC interview had said that his ability to pick pockets was a gift from God. He went on to say that he often preyed on unsuspecting Americans because "they are all rich." Some of John's associates had been robbed over the years. John was fortunate; it had not yet happened to him.

He turned the corner to see if the two men were still following. They were, so he darted into a bakery. The smell of pastries and freshly baked goods was mouth-watering. How often he had wished that he could find pastries like these in America.

John noticed that the men had stopped outside the door, waiting. John looked around the shop to see if there was another exit. He noticed a side door and walked out, careful to make sure the men did not see him. He continued to look behind him for several blocks and finally felt confident that he had lost them. He took a deep breath and continued looking for the restaurant.

He was unsure of whether he was going in the right direction since he had taken the detour through the bakery. He stopped several people to ask for directions before he found one who could speak English. He eventually found the place and was seated at a table with a good view of the street. He enjoyed watching the people pass by. After ordering a fish that sounded like sea bass, he relaxed and sipped a glass of Diet Coke, better known as cola light in Europe. The restaurant was decorated with beautiful paintings by local artists, many of which were for sale. He remembered that he still had the morning paper with him, so he opened it to the page with the photo of the green-eyed mystery lady. His waitress could speak a little English, so he asked her about the lady in the photo. "Oh sir," she explained, "she is one of our local TV news anchors. Her name is Ingrid Bauer. She is very famous here."

"Thanks," he said, as he wrote the name on the back of one of his business cards and put it in his wallet. After a nice dinner, John walked back to the hotel, intentionally going by the Pralinique shop just in case Ingrid might be there again, but not this time. The smell of fresh chocolate was so enticing that he went in and selected a variety of chocolates to take with him. As he walked on to the hotel munching on chocolate, he tried to figure out how he could see Ingrid again.

When John woke the next morning, he realized that it was Friday and tomorrow would begin another weekend for him away from home. After another busy workday, he caught a cab to the hotel and started packing an overnight bag for a weekend trip. John had decided to catch the train to Amsterdam. He had not been there in quite a while, and he always enjoyed the excitement of the bustling city.

Early the next morning, John walked to the train station, purchased a ticket at the automatic machine, and caught the express to Amsterdam. The view along the way was breathtaking. The countryside was dotted with small cottages, windmills, and dairy farms, most of them framed by a rainbow of tulips. Tulips everywhere, and they are so beautiful, he thought.

When he arrived in Amsterdam, he strolled to the center of the city. He was amazed at all the activities going on around him. The ancient stone streets had been in place for centuries, bordered by a river on one side and buildings on the other. The house where Ann Frank lived and wrote her diary in World War II was just down the street. Some of the buildings had survived the war, but many more had been destroyed. He thought about how magnificent

European cities would be today had World War II not taken place and destroyed so much. As he walked down the street, he saw a man in the city square stripping down to a G-string while a woman videotaped him performing a seductive dance. This kind of behavior was common in Amsterdam. Many people consider it to be the world's capital city of sin.

A few blocks further, John took a seat at a sidewalk café, ordered an espresso, and watched people passing on foot and bicycles. Bicycles were everywhere. Most of the locals used them as their primary means of transportation around the city.

Suddenly, a violent blast erupted and shook the ground under John's feet. He was stunned. Someone ran past him toward the train station yelling, "A bomb; it's a bomb."

He heard sirens and saw ambulances turning the corner. A bomb! Surely there weren't terrorist attacks here in Amsterdam.

John got up and walked around the corner and saw black smoke billowing from a shopping mall near the train station. Police were already on the scene and starting to tape off the area. Soon after, medics arrived and began helping the wounded. John saw the wreckage of a car that had been driven into the mall. It appeared to be the source of the bomb. The smell of explosives lingered in the air. Debris from the blast was scattered out into the street. People were crying, and workers were removing bodies on stretchers.

The site was total pandemonium. John turned to walk away and tripped over something. When he looked down, he discovered he had tripped over the body of a young woman. Her eyes were open with the blank stare of death and she was covered in blood. John felt the greatest sense of fear he could ever remember. How could this be; how could this kind of thing happen? Since the attack on the World Trade Center a few years ago, he knew no place in the world is totally safe, but this was so hard to witness.

John grabbed his overnight bag and walked several blocks to find a hotel – hopefully one on a side street where no car could drive into it. He finally found a place and sat for hours in his room, numbed by what he had just witnessed.

He picked up his cell phone, wanting to call someone back home for comfort. He stared at the phone as he thought about whom he could call. It finally occurred to him that there was no one at home he felt comfortable turning to for support at a time like this. He was suddenly overwhelmed by a feeling of loneliness. He put the phone down, looked at his watch, and decided to try to get some sleep.

Sometime later, he awoke to the sound of sirens wailing in the street, so he picked up the remote and turned on the TV. He wanted to see if the BBC might be reporting on the bombing. Thank God for BBC, a worldwide news service in English. **"Reporters are converging on Amsterdam from all parts of Europe. Hamas is suspected,"** the reporter was saying, **"however, no one has claimed responsibility at this point."**

Eventually John fell back to sleep but was again awakened by a nightmare about the woman whose body he had stumbled over at the site of bombing. He heard a noise outside his window, so he got up and walked over to look out. As he pulled back the curtain, he saw someone leading a woman down the sidewalk. She was bent over, sobbing. John wondered if she had lost a loved one in the bombing and thought about all the heartache in the world today. He went into the bathroom and splashed water on his face. Then, he decided that he would go back to the bombing site, mostly out of curiosity, but also because he was too keyed up to sleep.

He continued to listen to the BBC special report as he dressed to leave the hotel. They were reporting twenty-five people injured and at least fifteen more killed by the blast. Authorities were still sifting through rubble, and they expected those numbers would rise.

As John walked outside, it felt as though a chill had fallen over the shocked city. People seemed to be walking around aimlessly. The normal party atmosphere was gone. Police were everywhere, keeping an eye out for other attackers.

John walked past the house where Anne Frank and her family had lived while hiding from the Nazis. He saw the church on the corner with a small statue of her outside. He also saw the clock on the church that Anne looked at every day from her tiny bedroom window.

Anne Frank had lived in fear of an enemy that she could see. So many people today are terrorized by enemies that they can't see until it is too late. This city, like so many cities in our world, has seen its share of terror and fear.

John paused outside a large cathedral. He thought about how many beautiful churches he had seen while traveling the world. He slowly walked over to check the front door to see if it was unlocked. The knob turned easily. He stepped inside and paused while his eyes adjusted to the evening light coming through the stained-glass windows. Moving slowly, he walked to the front of the sanctuary, knelt at the communion table, and said a prayer for the innocent victims of the bombing and their families who were hurting so much tonight. He also said a prayer for himself – a prayer for direction, and guidance, and a prayer that he had prayed since childhood – a prayer that God would lead him to paradise in this world and the world to come. John had always believed that we could have a bit of paradise here on earth, but he also knew that it didn't come easy. He knew that it required a lot of work and a strong faith in God.

His mind wandered back to the memory of a large church he had seen in Strasburg, France a few years earlier. He had learned that it had taken over two hundred years to build that church. In his travels, he had seen many beautiful churches in many parts of the world. Some of them had beautiful, rare paintings and sculptures. He had seen one in Argentina that had amazing mosaic floors.

As John ended his prayer and reflection, he slowly got up and walked back out into the street. "Oh God," he whispered, "help me find your will for my life." My life has not been what either one of us wanted, he thought. I work, make a comfortable living, and save a little. But I want to feel I'm making a difference in this world.

John thought about how many times he had investigated the faces of corporate leaders over the years and said to them that they needed to find balance in their lives. How can I make that statement to others when I don't feel balanced in my own life? He thought about this more and more as he continued walking on to the scene of the bombing.

As John approached the site, he suddenly stopped and listened. He was certain he had heard a familiar voice. He looked in the direction where he thought he had heard it and his jaw dropped. There she was - Ingrid Bauer, the reporter from Belgium. She had probably taken a flight to get here to report on the bombing. He stared at her thinking, what is it about her? I don't even know this woman, and I am breathless when I see her. He watched, motionless. She was talking about the attack in a language that was foreign to him. John thought to himself, I wish I had studied more languages in high school and college. Spanish was not enough. I wish I could communicate in other languages with people that I meet and work with.

John waited several minutes for Ingrid to finish her report and get off camera. When she handed the mike back to her cameraman, she started to walk in his direction. He waited until she got closer and called out to her. "Ingrid!" He had no idea what to say when she stopped in front of him.

"Do I know you?" she asked.

"We met briefly in Belgium when we ran into each other at Pralinique Chocolate Shop. Do you have a few minutes? Would you like to get a cup of coffee?"

Ingrid looked around as she thought for a moment. At last, she said, "OK."

John went on. "I saw your picture in the newspaper and learned your name after running into you at Pralinique. My name is John Martin."

"Hi John," she said as she extended her hand and shook his. "I do remember almost running over you coming out of the candy shop. I am so sorry."

"No need to apologize," he said. "You made quite an impression on me." Ingrid blushed slightly and smiled as they sat down at a small table outside a coffee shop. "I just wanted someone to talk to. This bombing has been so disturbing," John said. He looked at her for a moment lost in her eyes, almost missing her response.

"Yes, it is frightening. It seems there are no

safe places left in our world today. Did you see what happened?" she asked in her reporter tone of voice. "No," he replied. "I was around the corner when I heard the blast. So, I ran to see what the noise was and stumbled over a body." He ran his fingers through his hair as he continued. "There were so many injured people and such chaos that I didn't know what to do. When the police arrived, we were all forced to move back while they taped off the scene."

Ingrid didn't say anything, but her eyes spoke volumes about her concern and shock.

"After a while, I left to find a hotel and watched news reports on the bombing. I finally decided to come back here to see the extent of the damage for myself. I only came to Amsterdam for the weekend and never expected to witness such an event. And I especially didn't expect to run into you here."

They ordered coffee and sat in silence for a while. When the coffee arrived, they sipped on it and spoke little. The small cups of espresso were so strong that John had to add some hot water to weaken it. The shop was cozy and overlooked the river running through the city. John was so lost in Ingrid's beauty that he struggled to think about what to say.

Ingrid said, "This reminds me of a bombing I reported on a couple of years ago. I think this one is worse because there are more victims."

"I don't know how you do it. I don't think I could stand to see the devastation and loss that you must see often in your work," he responded.

"John, you are obviously an American. Where is your home?" she asked.

"I grew up in a small town in Montana, went away

to college in Colorado, fell in love with the Rocky Mountains, and settled there," he replied. "I always enjoyed traveling, so I chose a profession that would allow me to travel. As a result, I've seen a great deal of the world. However, I still love to go home to the Rockies and relax. Amsterdam is one of my favorite cities to visit, so here I am," he continued.

"Yes," she said slowly, "here you are." Before she could say anything more, her cell phone started ringing. One of the worst inventions of our lives, John thought. Ingrid closed her phone. "Well thanks for the coffee, John. I must go. They want an update. It was nice talking to you."

With that she got up and headed for the sidewalk. She turned and gave him a smile and a slight wave. John was disappointed. He wanted more time to talk to her. He wanted to get her phone number and arrange a meeting later. But she was gone just as quickly as she was at the chocolate shop a few days earlier.

He thought, what is so compelling about her? He believed from his years of studying psychology and personalities that she was a loving, compassionate person; the kind of woman he had always been attracted to. He could hear it in her voice and see it in her eyes. He could tell by their brief encounter that she was an unusual and special woman. Yet they were so different, he thought. John felt he was so logical, rational, and mechanical. She functioned so much more on a human level. Maybe that is why I have been so lonely, he thought to himself. Perhaps I need a higher level of sensitivity in my life. Women seem to want men to be more sensitive, he mused.

John watched as Ingrid disappeared into the crowd. He finally got up and walked down the street by the same town square where a few hours earlier a man had stripped in front of his lover's camera. The square was now filled with young people milling around. Since drugs were legal here, it was not uncommon to see people stoned out of their minds. Drug deals occurred on a regular basis in public.

As he was leaving the site of the bombing, police and rescue personnel were encouraging people to leave the area and giving instructions on what to do if they were trying to get information regarding loved ones. They weren't letting anyone near the scene.

It was getting late so John headed back to the hotel. His room contained a small TV, bed, and nightstand. Not many creature comforts here, he thought.

The next morning, the sun was shining brightly through the window of his hotel room when he woke up. Sunday morning in Amsterdam - the sky was blue, the tulips were in bloom, and the street was quiet. John walked over to the window. He noticed how much litter remained in the streets after all the upheaval the night before. The garbage collection carts were overflowing with beer bottles. Very few people were in the streets; only a few were riding bicycles at this early hour. John was always amazed at how many people in Holland rode bicycles.

John decided that he would like to attend a worship service, so he looked through the local phone book and found the address of a church that appeared to be close to the hotel. He remembered how churches had been filled after the attack on the World Trade Center in New York. He wondered if the same thing would occur here. After showering, he headed to the hotel's front desk to get directions. As he walked through the streets on this crisp, clear morning he was aware that the peace and presence of God seemed to surround everything.

He found the church. Its beautiful architecture was very impressive. As he entered the sanctuary, he walked across lovely mosaic floors. He picked up a headset so he could hear the service in English from a translator and took a seat where he could have a view of the entire room. The service had not begun, so he bowed his head and started to pray. "God, please give me balance in my life." He had decided that he needed a greater sense of purpose and meaning in his life other than work. **"Work should not be the number one thing in a person's life,"** he thought.

While he was contemplating this, John felt that God was speaking to him and reminding him that balance was something he really could control. He should learn to prioritize how he spent his time between work, family, community, and his spiritual life. And of course, he needed to spend time taking care of himself – exercising and doing things that were important to him. This was the area of his life that he usually neglected. As he left the church, John realized that the bombing apparently had little impact on people's need for spiritual support. The church was not very crowded. It looked like the usual small group he had always seen in European churches. After the service, he went back to the hotel to check out and then headed for the train station. It was time for him to head back to Belgium and to work.

The train ride back to Bruges was uneventful. As he looked out the window, he saw lots of small farms with large windmills in historic towns. He wished that he had more time to visit this area. As he thought more about it, he decided it was time to take some measure of control of his life. He got off the train at the next stop in the town of Haarlem, Holland. He wanted to visit a place that he had read about many years earlier called the Beje, or the Hiding Place.

Since 1837, the Ten Boom family had operated a clock and watch shop on a street corner in this town. Descendants of that family - Corrie Ten Boom, her sister Betsie, and their father Casper
- had created a small hiding place in their upstairs living quarters where they hid Jews from the Nazi Gestapo during World War II. Eventually, the family was discovered and captured and sent to a Nazi concentration camp called Ravensbruck. Corrie survived Ravensbruck, but all her family members perished. Corrie traveled the world after the war to the keep alive the spiritual heritage of the Ten Boom family and their love for God and His people.

John took a cab and stopped close to the Beje. He got out and walked down the street in the direction of the watch shop. On the way, he entered a nearby cheese shop and sampled some of the world's greatest cheeses. He wished there was a way to have some of the cheeses shipped home to Colorado but knew it would be too difficult.

As John walked into the clock and watch shop, he learned that the Ten Boom family no longer owned it. However, the current owners had kept the shop much like it had been during the war. The upstairs living quarters had been preserved in its original condition for almost two hundred years and were open to public viewing. John paid the small fee and walked upstairs. He was amazed at the small size of the Hiding Place, but he felt a special connection to God as he viewed the place that had provided safety for so many Jewish people so that their lives were spared.

An hour later, John boarded the train and once again headed for Belgium. He felt so renewed for having taken the time along the way to follow one of his long-hoped-for plans.

Back in Belgium the next morning, John woke at dawn ready to get back to work. He found it difficult to concentrate on the problems of the company. His mind kept drifting back to the weekend in Amsterdam. And, of course, the short time he had spent with Ingrid at the coffee shop.

The remainder of the week was uneventful and when Friday arrived, he started the long trip home to Colorado. As he heard the clang of the airplane wheels folding into the belly of the plane, his mind was filled with thoughts of Ingrid. Would he ever see her again? He decided he would look for the phone number of her company and attempt to call her.

CHAPTER 2 – JOHN & INGRID

After a very long flight, John arrived at the airport in Denver. He caught the airport shuttle to his Jeep in a distant corner of long-term parking. When he turned on the car's ignition, John Denver was singing, "Country roads, take me home, to the place where I belong." He had been listening to the CD when he had driven to the airport so many days ago. John joined in and started singing at the top of his voice. He pointed the Jeep in the direction of the Rocky Mountains and accelerated toward home in the mountains that he loved.

On the way to his house, John stopped at the kennel where he had boarded his two dogs. He walked in and waited for Denise, the owner, to get off the phone. After a couple of minutes, she hung up and said, "Hello John! Glad you're home safe. Let me get your boys for you."

"Thanks," he replied. "I am anxious to see them and get them home." He heard their feet tapping and scratching the floor as they dragged Denise down the hall. Duke, a golden retriever, and Bear, a shepherd mix, leaped for John when they came around the corner. John knelt and rubbed their heads and ears for a couple of minutes before taking their leashes and heading for the Jeep. The dogs jumped in, pushing each other for access to the front seat. They settled down after Duke won the seat battle and Bear took a seat on the floor. John closed the door and went back inside to pay and make sure they were booked for his next trip. "See you in a couple of days," he said as he walked out to the Jeep where his buddies were waiting patiently for him.

As he started the Jeep, both dogs tried to lay their heads on his leg and look contented as the trio headed for the home they all loved. When he pulled into the driveway,

John paused and said a prayer of thanks to be home again. When he opened the door, the dogs leaped out and started running through the yard, chasing each other. John unloaded the Jeep and let the dogs play until they exhausted themselves.

It was chilly in the house, so he got a fire started in the fireplace and adjusted the thermostat. Next, he went into the kitchen to see what he could find to cook. He had always enjoyed being an amateur chef, but he was so tired from the trip that tonight he decided to settle for heating a frozen dinner. After taking it out of the microwave, John sat down at the table by the window that overlooked a small stream flowing out of the mountain. It was always tough to eat alone, and it seemed that he had spent most of his adult life eating alone or with business associates. John longed to eat with a woman who shared his life and someone who would appreciate this beautiful place. His mind immediately wandered to Ingrid. Where was she? What was she doing? Would he ever see her again?

He noticed a couple of mule deer wandering into the yard as he finished his meal. They enjoyed nibbling the grass and the flowers he had planted in the spring. Duke and Bear came bounding around the corner of the house to claim their territory. The deer leaped back into the trees and disappeared. John always loved this place because of its natural beauty and the wildlife that constantly paraded by his windows. "Thank you, God," he whispered. He put the dishes in the dishwasher, brought the dogs inside, and headed for his favorite chair in front of a large flat screen TV. Within a few minutes he had fallen asleep. He woke up a couple of hours later, fed the dogs, and headed for bed.

The next morning John woke up with the sun

shining through the bedroom windows. He dressed and fed the dogs. After letting them outside, he headed for the small gym in his basement. He got on the treadmill, turned on Fox News, and started his workout routine. After an hour of walking, lifting weights, and stretching, he got into the sauna for a short while and then headed for the shower. It was tough to maintain a regular exercise routine, especially on the road, but he always felt much better after he exercised.

After he was dressed, he grabbed an apple and headed for his home office to check email. When he looked at his watch a couple of hours later, he realized how lost he had become in work once again. He knew that if he was ever going to maintain a work-life balance, he had to force himself into some new behaviors. He got up, put on a jacket, and went outside to play with the dogs.

John felt so lonely at times like this. He longed for someone special to share his life with. Again, he said a prayer, a longer prayer than usual. It was so easy and natural to talk to God here in this place of beauty and natural serenity.

He then decided to go to the grocery store a few miles away to pick up a few things. He stopped at a gas station first to fill up, and then drove on to the grocery store. He picked up a few essential items - some food for his upcoming trip and some treats for the dogs. As he strolled down the aisles, he looked at each woman's face wishing he could see Ingrid. He finished his shopping and headed home.

On the drive home, he started preparing for his upcoming trip to Indonesia. It could take as long as thirty to thirty-six hours to get there from Colorado depending on the route taken. He had to do some laundry and pack clothing for hot weather. John remembered how hot it was as he walked off the plane the last time he was there. He immediately felt the hot humid heat as he walked through the jet way and into the airport. He would also need to stop by the bank on the way to the airport and pick up some new $100 bills. The Indonesians don't want to exchange for old worn money. They want new bills that have no folds or marks on them. They think Americans are terrible for writing on their currency.

John's flight to Asia would leave at midnight from LAX, so he would need to be at the airport by early evening to ensure that his luggage would get from one plane to the other. By mid-morning, he had loaded his luggage, the dogs, and work materials he would need and departed his mountain retreat. He dropped off the dogs with Denise and stopped by the bank before heading to the Denver airport.

His flight from Denver was uneventful, but the flight on China Air to Jakarta was always difficult because of the long lines waiting to board the plane. People shuffled bags along the line to check in. It could take hours to get to the counter to check in and get through security. There were few frequent flier advantages anymore with the airlines, so trying to get an aisle seat, which he preferred, would be a challenge. He prayed that he would not get stuck in a middle seat for the long, boring flight.

John was exhausted by the time he finally got to the gate where he would board. He dropped into a seat and dozed while waiting for the boarding to begin. When his turn came to board, he was fortunate to get an aisle seat. At least he would be able to get up and stretch occasionally during the flight. John's luck held and no one else was assigned to his row, so after the flight was in the air, he lay down across the three seats and fell asleep.

While he slept, he dreamed about Ingrid and he woke up thinking about her. He remembered that he had meant to look for her company phone number and call her. Once again, he had gotten so caught up in preparing for work and business travel that he had forgotten about his more important personal plans.

John changed planes in Hong Kong and continued to Jakarta. When he finally arrived in Jakarta, he was anxious to get to a hotel to take a shower. As he left the plane, he was again aware of the heat. He stopped at Customs, pulled out his passport, and prayed that he wouldn't have to pay a bribe to get through. People in Jakarta were very poor and many of them were so corrupt that they found tourists to be easy targets. Once John had convinced the Customs officials that he was in Jakarta on business and not as a tourist, he could enter the country.

John had a friend named Samuel whom he had met many years earlier when Samuel attended college in America. John and Samuel had decided to meet at the airport. As John passed through security, he started looking through the crowd for his friend. He finally saw Samuel, a very short Asian man, waving at him.

“I am happy to see you again,” Samuel said with a huge smile

“And I am happy to see you, my friend,” John replied.

Samuel, like many citizens of Jakarta, had a driver.

The driver would take John and Samuel to John's

hotel.

“There is no way I would ever want to drive in this country," he said to Samuel. "This is one of the toughest cities in the world to get around in.”

The streets were crowded with cars, sport utility vehicles, trucks, buses, motorcycles, and three-wheeled vehicles called Bajaj, all moving at a snail's pace just inches apart from each other on both sides, front, and back. There are no air pollution standards in this country, so exhaust from the various vehicles is so thick that most people wear handkerchiefs over their mouths and noses to try to protect themselves.

At every intersection, children came up to their vehicle begging for a few coins. Women holding babies that they may have rented from mothers came up, banging on the windows asking for money. Poverty was rampant. Children and adults were trying to sell all kinds of food and trinkets to people in every vehicle. It was a congested nightmare. It could take hours to get through the traffic to the hotel.

John thought the people of Jakarta were very nice. They are kind, gentle people in the middle of one of the worst terrorist hotbeds of the world, he thought. He knew that there were many radical religious groups here, and there was a lot of violence and radical activities going on all the time. Riots break out frequently. Hotels where Americans tend to stay are often targeted for bombings. The radical groups are filled with hatred for Americans, and especially Americans who are Christians. Christian churches are often burned, and thousands of Christians have been killed by radical Muslim groups.

As they crawled through traffic, John whispered a prayer. "I am so thankful to be an American and to live in a country that still allows religious freedom. With all the problems in America, it is still the greatest nation in the world," he thought.

They finally arrived at the Hotel Santika. As they pulled up at the entrance, guards were standing at the gate to search all vehicles as they entered. They ran mirrors under the car looking for bombs. They looked inside at all the passengers, looking for people who might be terrorists. After the search, John and Samuel drove up to the front entrance to check in. Samuel could speak several languages fluently and served as John's interpreter. John was able to get checked in quickly. The Santika was one of John's favorite places to stay since it included exercise facilities and massages for about $10. In the U.S., the same spa treatment would cost about $100.

There was an eleven-hour time difference between Indonesia and Colorado, and John was very tired from the long trip, so he went to bed early. He had a busy schedule planned for the next day working with a group of leaders in a company that manufactured anti-terrorism detection devices. With Indonesia being so far behind the rest of the world in technology, he was surprised to find a company like this one here.

Indonesia has almost no human resource laws to protect its workers. Managers are often rude and even brutal to employees. If a worker is injured, they are simply fired and replaced. John's client company wanted to expand into international sales, so they knew they had to train their managers to treat people better and be able to prove to international buyers that they treat their employees humanely.

John loved shopping in Jakarta since there were so many unique items available. Prices were much lower than in other parts of the world, and the dollar is worth much more in Indonesia. Gold jewelry was less expensive than most places in the world. John found himself wanting to buy something for Ingrid. He negotiated on a 24-carat gold bracelet with the hopes of giving it to her at some point after he returned to Belgium.

After three days of intense management and

leadership training, John was ready to leave Jakarta. The people of Indonesia were so wonderful to work with, but they lived and worked in a land of few creature comforts. As he rode through the city, John saw people hanging out of shabby buses with no doors. Trash littered the streets and rivers. The people had to fight to survive day to day. If only the government were not so corrupt and would take better care of its citizens, he wished.

On his way to the airport, John thought about Ingrid and his great desire to find a soul mate. For several years, he had hoped to meet someone special with whom to share his life. He had met so many wonderful people as he traveled the world, but the love of his life had been elusive. There had been Katherine, but he could not allow himself to think about her now.

Once again John was heading home to Colorado. He had a layover in Singapore, one of the cleanest cities in Asia where there were severe fines for littering. He spent the night in a downtown hotel since his flight was not until the following day. After dinner, he went for a walk. Again, he found himself thinking about Ingrid, and he decided that he would call her when he got home.

Three days later he arrived in Denver. He went to the kennel to pick up his buddies. After getting home, he had the usual battle with jet lag. It was always harder coming back home than going away, and it usually took a couple of days to get back to normal.

John decided to take the dogs for a walk in the mountains. It was chilly this time of year but after a brisk walk he was feeling invigorated. The jet lag was gone, and the snow-covered Rockies were so beautiful. The dogs bounded along the trail chasing rabbits.

John always felt close to God when he got out in nature. It was a great time to pray. He had learned to talk to God as though he were talking to a good friend. At times, he struggled with hearing God whisper to him since those whispers can come when we least expect them. He constantly prayed for God's guidance and direction, but at times it seemed that God was silent. During those silent times, John persisted in his faith that God was there listening. It wasn't always easy, but it was the only thing he knew to do. He had once been told that **"faith was reaching out into the unknown and getting hold of that which was not and holding on until it became that which is."** It sounded simple, but it was not easy. John knew that his faith in God had sustained him throughout his life, and he completely trusted Jesus Christ in every way.

John thought about all the religions he had witnessed in different parts of the world. He knew that religions were often used in dangerous ways. But he also knew that the only thing that mattered was a personal relationship with Jesus Christ.

John had been looking forward to going back to Belgium for several days as he now prepared for the trip. The day before, he had searched the internet and found Ingrid's work phone number. He dialed the number to ask for her and was delighted to hear her voice on the other end of the call. Because of the six-hour time difference, he caught her just before she was to leave for the day.

"Hi, Ingrid. This is John Martin."

She was silent for a moment then said, "You're the gentleman I had coffee with in Amsterdam."

"Yes," he replied. "I am coming to Belgium next week, and I wanted to know if we could have dinner one night?"

After a long pause she said, "I feel like that would be OK. Why don't you call me when you get here, and we will decide when and where to meet, is that OK?" she asked.

"That would be great. I will call you on Tuesday. What is the best number to reach you?" he asked.

After exchanging cell phone numbers, they ended the conversation. John was breathless and so glad he had placed the call. "Thank you, God," he whispered.

For the first time in a long time, he was excited to get on an airplane for the nine-hour trip across the Atlantic Ocean. As the plane left the ground, he remembered the words from TV he had heard as a child. "Up, up, and away." He was too excited to sleep, so after dinner he read for a while to try to relax. He knew he would need to be rested when he arrived. The work would be exhausting. He had read once that one hour of public speaking was the equivalent of eight hours of manual labor. He believed it to be true, especially as he grew older.

When the plane landed, he joined the long line going through customs, explained his reason for being there, and then rushed to pick up his rental car. Sometime later, he was pulling into his hotel parking lot in Bruges. After getting settled in his room, he made sure that he had all the materials organized that he would need the next day.

The alarm sounded early the next morning. He

got dressed and went downstairs for a European breakfast of cheeses, lunch meats, pastries, and fruit. He could hardly wait to call Ingrid. Just before leaving the hotel, he called her and arranged a time and location for dinner. Now he was even more excited. It was going to be a great day. He walked into the client's office to set up for the workshop.

Ingrid had suggested that they meet at 6:30 that evening at a nice French restaurant that she thought would be appropriate for their first date. John arrived a few minutes early. He was so anxious to see her again and was delighted to see that she was there already. Maybe that is a good sign, he thought. Maybe she is as anxious as I am. At least he hoped so.

"Hello, Ingrid. You look lovely tonight," he said and sincerely meant it. "Thank you, John. It is good to see you again," she replied.

"This is a very nice place," he said. "It smells wonderful." She smiled, "I am glad you like it. It is one of my favorite places. I come here every chance I get." She continued, "Most tourists don't know about this place since it is on a small side street, so it is usually quiet here."

They ordered and settled into small talk. Eventually, their conversation progressed to more serious topics. Time flew by and before they knew it three hours had passed. It seemed that neither of them wanted to leave, but finally Ingrid said she better leave since she needed to get an early start the next morning. John reluctantly agreed and suggested that they have dinner again the next night. Ingrid quickly agreed. John paid the bill and walked her down the street.

They passed a sidewalk vendor who was selling

flowers. “A rose for the lady,” the vendor said. John purchased one and handed it to Ingrid. “It is customary to give the lady a kiss when you give her a rose,” the vendor said. With great joy, John complied and kissed Ingrid gently on the lips. She didn’t seem to mind.

At the door of her flat, they again exchanged a short kiss, agreed on a time and location for dinner the next evening, and said goodnight. John felt he was walking on clouds as he headed to his hotel. Maybe, he thought, just maybe, this was the one he had been waiting for all these years. Maybe, just maybe, she would become the love of his life. He had trouble sleeping because he couldn't stop thinking about her.

The next evening, they ate at an Italian restaurant and enjoyed some Italian food. Their conversation picked up where it had left off the night before. When they left the restaurant, they walked down the sidewalk toward the canal that flowed through the city. They held hands as they walked along. When they saw a paddle boat dock, they decided to go for a ride on the canal. As they settled into the boat, John pulled Ingrid close hoping to keep her warm and silently thanked God for what was happening with this lovely lady. The pilot paddled slowly along the shore of the city. The city lights shimmered in the water, creating a beautiful background for the romantic ride.

“I’m so glad I am here with you,” John said. “It's nice to have someone to talk to."

"I am glad we are here too,” Ingrid replied.

They floated by several cathedrals with the light shining through their stained-glass windows. The aromas from the nearby restaurants created a pleasant fragrance. John hardly noticed any of those things.

His gaze was fixed on the beautiful lady in his arms. This only happens in movies, he thought as he noticed the wonderful fragrance of her perfume.

An hour later, they got off the boat and continued their stroll toward Ingrid's apartment. As they walked down the street, they noticed an artist near the canal painting a scene of the city. The artist had a stack of finished paintings in a box beside him. “Would you like to buy a painting?" he asked. They looked through the box and picked one for each of them.

"When we look at these paintings in our homes, we will think of this night and each other,” Ingrid suggested.

“Yes,” he said. “I will never forget this night.”

They walked the rest of the way and embraced as they said goodnight. John caught a cab back to the hotel. In his room, he looked at the painting and thought about this night and the beautiful lady who was quickly stealing his heart.

They saw each other several more times during the remainder of that week. During John's second week in Belgium they saw each other every night. He no longer felt like this trip was for work. He looked forward to each day and spending more time with Ingrid.

John was only scheduled to be in Belgium for two weeks, so it was time for him to leave for home. His client always wanted to get as much out of him as they could on these trips since his travel expenses from the U.S. were quite high. As John and Ingrid grew closer each day, he began wishing he were staying in Belgium longer. They walked around the city for hours each evening. They sat on a park bench in the city square holding hands and talking. As they had dinner on their last evening together, he gave her the bracelet he had purchased for her in Indonesia.

"Oh, John! Thank you. It is a very beautiful gift, and I will always think of you when I wear it," she said.

As they said goodnight, they held each other for a long time. This is too painful, he thought. He could not remember caring for anyone this much. It hurts to be away from the person you love, and it hurts not to have someone to love. So, which would you choose? he asked himself.

John whispered, "I'll be back in a month. I hope we can continue to get to know each other then."

"I will be counting the days," she said. They promised to email and phone each other daily. Finally, he kissed her goodnight and stood for a long moment after she closed the door. He decided to walk back to the hotel and take in the scenes of the city one more time before he left. This is the first time in a long time that he did not want to go home. He wished there was a way to stay here with her forever. A month is not too long, he thought. I'll be busy, and it will go by quickly.

Ingrid stood inside her flat with her heart pounding as she heard him walk away. She wondered how she would make it until they could see each other again. She thought that this was possibly the greatest love she had ever known. She did not want him to leave. Suddenly, she froze as she remembered that she had requested a job transfer some time ago. She hoped it would not come through. She had no idea at the time she submitted her request that she would meet a man who was possibly the greatest love of her life.

"Oh, God," she prayed. "Please don't let the transfer happen. But not my will but Your will be done. You know what is best."

As she turned and walked to her bedroom, it seemed as though every step she took was more difficult. Her heart was aching, and the future seemed so uncertain. Perhaps she should tell John about the possibility of a transfer, but it might not happen. Surely it won't happen in the next month, she thought. She finally fell asleep thinking about him.

John was standing in the airport waiting for the call to board his flight to the U.S. As soon as he heard the wheels clank in the bottom of the plane, he fell asleep.

He followed his usual routine when he returned home with one exception; he missed Ingrid and couldn't stop thinking about her. He found it difficult to do his work. He longed for the next opportunity for them to talk or email each other.

When he had been home for a week, he received an email from her that caused him to sit back in his chair and close his eyes. No, no, he said to himself. This can't happen.

"John" she wrote, "I am being transferred to the Fox News office in Jerusalem. I will be leaving within the next two weeks. The former correspondent there was killed a few days ago in a bombing, and they want me there right away. I had requested a promotional assignment several months ago, and now I regret it. At the time I made the request, I had no idea I would meet someone like you and how that would change my plans. But now I really have no choice. I hope we can still find a way to see each other soon."

He immediately picked up the phone and called her. The hour was late, but he wanted her to know that he understood and that he was committed to the relationship and that somehow, they would find a way to see each other. They both had tears in their eyes when they hung up the phone, and they both understood that somehow love would find a way.

"You have the business card I gave you before you left. It has my cell phone number on it. That number won't change, and

you can call it any time. I have your number, too. So, we will continue to talk and email every day," she said.

As they hung up, John wondered how he could arrange to see her again. Israel was a long way from the U.S. After a long time, he finally fell asleep. It was not a restful night. He found it impossible to get her out of his mind. This was not going to be an easy transition.

CHAPTER 3 - INGRID

Ingrid was having the same problem as John. She tossed and turned. What it is about this man, she asked herself. No one had ever impacted her like that. No one had ever stolen her heart like he had and certainly not so quickly.

The next morning, Ingrid moved around in a daze. She busied herself with cleaning her apartment, but still could not concentrate. She wished she could tell him how much he meant to her. She thought about how she should have told him that she loved him because she knew in her heart that they both felt the same way. There are never adequate words to express your feelings when love between two people is so perfect. I was a journalism major but found it impossible to come up with the words to express what is in my heart, she thought.

Her mind wandered back to her youth to a simpler time and a much simpler place. She had grown up in one of the most beautiful, and one of the smallest, countries in Europe. She had grown up in Ettelbruck, Luxembourg in a family of educators. Her father was a college professor at the University of Antwerp before his death five years earlier. Her mother still lived there and was a poet and author, thus Ingrid's interest in journalism and writing.

As a teen, Ingrid's parents had survived the German occupation and the intense bombing of Ettelbruck and the surrounding area near the Battle of the Bulge. It was a time when the beautiful green meadows were turned into fields of snow, mud, and blood as the Allied troops marched and fought during the winter months.

Ingrid remembered fondly the statue of General

George Armstrong Patton and the American tank and flag that greeted all visitors to her hometown even to this day. Her dad had often talked about the liberation in December of 1944 and of his appreciation for the Americans who fought and died to liberate them from the Germans.

Much of Ettelbruck had to be rebuilt after the war. Ingrid's home at the time was on the main street of town in a three-story flat that Americans called apartments or townhouses. Her bedroom was on the top floor. As a young girl, she remembered looking out of her window and dreaming of falling in love with a handsome man. John fulfilled her childhood dreams. She realized that the love she felt for him was the love she had dreamed about. She had never loved anyone like this before and found it hard to believe that it was possible. Again, she thought how much she wished she had told him how much she cared for him. She didn't understand why it was so difficult for her to express her emotions.

She thought about her years in college at the University of Antwerp and the first man she thought she had been in love with. They had dated for three years, and she thought they would eventually get married. She had always enjoyed walking the streets of Antwerp with him. They enjoyed sitting in sidewalk cafés and coffee shops, and they would talk for hours. She had always loved the quaint feel of it. Today, Antwerp is a very cosmopolitan city with all the modern shops that baby boomers and generation X'ers frequented.

Shortly after their engagement, she had gone by her fiancé's flat to pick up a textbook she had forgotten. She was devastated to find him in the bed with her best friend. The pain was still there when she thought about his betrayal. She still remembered the shock on their faces when they realized that she was in the room. She heard them calling her name as she tossed the engagement ring on the bed and left, slamming the door behind her. They never talked again.

"Time does not heal all wounds," her dad always told her. "Only God heals, my child," he would say. She now realized how right he was. When she allowed her mind to wander back to painful events, she felt much the same pain as when the event occurred. She said to herself, "I must put the past out of my mind and live for the future." Maybe the pain of the past was what had kept her from expressing her true emotions. Maybe there was still some fear of getting hurt again.

Life is a risk. There is always the possibility of getting hurt when imperfect people fall in love. So, you either take the risk or you may never know the joy of true love. Maybe she was too trusting, but she would rather trust and risk than become hardhearted and suspicious.

After college, Ingrid had worked for a local newspaper called the *LUXEMBOURG WORT*. Soon after, she got a job as a reporter for a nearby Belgium TV station. Three years later, she got a call from Fox News. "Would you be interested in serving as our correspondent in Luxembourg and the Ardennes?" the caller from New York asked. She had accepted the offer almost immediately. She had now worked for two years with Fox in Luxembourg and a year on assignment in Bruges, Belgium.

A few days after John left, her boss Wilhelm

called her into his office and told her that her request had been granted. “We need you to replace our correspondent in Jerusalem, Israel right away. The correspondent there was killed suddenly in a bombing attack on the hotel he was staying in.”

She was speechless for a moment before she finally said, "Jerusalem. Wow. I never expected a Middle East assignment. I was expecting to go somewhere in Europe.”

“I know,” Wilhelm said. “But you are good at reporting on bombings and violent incidents. We saw that in Amsterdam. We really need you to go. There is no one else that has the flexibility and availability that you have."

“OK,” she replied. “I will arrange to go right away.” “Thanks,” said Wilhelm.

With that, she left his office and walked slowly back to hers, running her fingers through her hair. This was not what she had expected. She sat down at her computer and stared at it for several minutes, then finally sent an email to John.

She then picked up the phone and called her mother in Luxembourg. “Hi, Mum. Guess what. I am being transferred to Jerusalem.” Her mother did not reply for a few moments, and then she said slowly, “Jerusalem. Will you be safe there?”

“Oh, Mum – I will be fine. But I do have some apprehensions about leaving Belgium just now,” she said, not wanting her mother to worry. But as always, she did not hide anything from her mother.

They talked for a long time about the trip, and finally Ingrid told her mother about John. Her mom listened and said “He sounds wonderful. I will keep you in my prayers. I love you, dear.”

"I love you too, Mum. I will be home to spend a couple of days with you before I leave for Jerusalem, and I will leave my car with you. Talk to you soon."

"I can't wait to see you. I will tell your sister so you can spend some time with her and the children while you are here."

After hanging up, Ingrid felt better. She always did after talking to her mother. So many times, her mother had prayed for her. She remembered coming home late at night when she was in high school and her mother would be waiting for her. "I have been praying for you tonight," she would say.

John's phone call was comforting and reassuring when they talked later. She could hear the sadness and concern in his voice, but he said all the right words. It made her love him even more. She thought again about how John was such a special and unusual man.

Three days later, she was packing her car and getting ready to leave her flat in Belgium. After loading most of her belongings in her old BMW convertible, she headed toward Ettelbruck and its beautiful countryside. She had never been to Israel, but she had heard that it was very rocky and rough compared to the beautiful green meadows of this part of Europe. There was so much history here and there. It was hard to imagine how devastated this area was during World War II. She wished she had time to stop at Bourscheid Castle that overlooked the river, but she knew it would take too long. There are many places in Europe where people can drive by a castle on a nearby hillside. Ingrid remembered reading about a castle in America that was built by the Vanderbilt family, but she could not remember where it was located.

She was anxious to get to her family home and spend as much time as possible with her mother. Her dad had died the year before, but she knew he would be pleased that she was involved with an American. He had always said, "Thanks to America, we are free from the Nazi domination. We learned to appreciate freedom." She thought about him sitting in his favorite chair in the evening, smoking his pipe and reflecting on how much he appreciated living in a free country again. "Only those who have lived through such a nightmare can truly know how horrible it is," he often reflected.

As she got close to home, she decided to roll down the windows. She would have put the top down, but the car was packed too full. She enjoyed the sight of sheep grazing on the hillsides and the smell of the countryside. It felt good to be going home as she drove a little faster. This country is so small, and most tourists don't know that it is one of the most beautiful places in Europe. It is one-fifth the size of England. It has its own wine country, Abby towns, a cosmopolitan city, hiking trails, restored castles, beautiful rivers, and lovely people who are bi-lingual and multicultural. "Thank you, God, for letting me grow up here," she whispered.

When she arrived home, she quickly parked on the street. She remembered that when she was in training in the United States for her job, most people parked in driveways and garages. Not in Europe. Here, most people parked on the street if they could find an open spot. She wondered what John's home was like in the Rocky Mountains. She thought she would look it up on Google Earth when she got her computer setup.

Ingrid was so anxious to see her mother that

she almost ran from the car to the front door. Bounding up the steps from the street, she took them two at a time and opened the door. "Mum, I'm home," she called out. "Mum, where are you?" she asked, not waiting for an answer.

"Here, baby. I am in the kitchen." Ingrid rushed into the kitchen noticing the pleasant smell of food cooking and grabbed her mother in a bear hug. She almost stepped on their family dog, Shadow, a poodle, who immediately darted under the table to avoid being stepped on.

Ingrid and her mother embraced for a long time. Her mother's embrace made her feel so safe – no bombs, no violence; only love and serenity. Her mother placed her favorite pasta dish on the table. The smell of tomato sauce and parmesan cheese made her mouth water. They sat down and ate and talked for several hours. It was almost midnight when Ingrid stretched and said to her mother, "I'd better get my things out of the car and let you get some rest." She headed out to the car and grabbed her overnight bag.

Her mother had rushed up to her old room, turned down the bed, and sat waiting for her. "Let me help you put your things away," she said as she grabbed the overnight bag and carried it into the bathroom.

"Thanks, Mum," she said.

It was 10:00 am the next morning when her eyes opened. She looked at the clock in disbelief. "Oh, dear," she said to herself. "I am sleeping the day away." It had been a long time since she had slept so long. She could smell the aroma of coffee drifting up the stairs as she headed down.

She hugged her mother. “Good morning, dear,” her mother said as Ingrid sat down at the table.

“I'm sorry I slept so long. You should have called me,” she said.

“No. You needed to rest. You have a long, hard journey ahead of you.”

Ingrid poured a cup of coffee and held it in her hands to warm them. The house was a little chilly this morning. Her mother pushed a plate of pastries, cheese, and ham toward Ingrid. She immediately started to eat. “I guess I was hungrier than I realized,” she said as she ate a pastry.

“Your sister is on her way over. She phoned a few minutes ago. She'll be here soon.”

“Wonderful! I'm so anxious to see her.”

Rebecca rushed in a few moments later. She was pregnant and carrying her three-year-old. They greeted each other with big hugs. Rebecca was married to Eric who worked at one of the local banks. They had three children already and another on the way.

They talked over cups of coffee, sharing and catching up on each other's lives. Rebecca was surprised to learn that Ingrid was going to Israel.

“Are you sure you will be safe?” she wanted to know.

“I will be careful, I'll be working with a camera crew, so I should be alright,” Ingrid replied.

Ingrid thought for a moment. “Mum, Rebecca. I want to tell you about a man I met in Belgium – an American. He is so nice and has become very special to me.” They listened intently as she talked about her relationship with John. Rebecca looked at her mother and said, “Look at her. Have you ever seen her light up like this before when talking about a man? This must be serious.” Ingrid blushed.

After lunch Rebecca said, “I hate to leave you two, but the kids will be getting home from school soon. I’ll call you in the morning.” She left holding the hand of her three-year-old who tried to run ahead.

Ingrid felt so lonely after her sister left. They had always been close and now they had so little time together. She wished she could be here to watch the children grow. She would soon be so far away.

She put on her jacket and said to her mother, “I'm going for a walk before dinner. I’ll be back soon.”

Ingrid walked past the International School of Luxembourg, her old high school. She looked fondly at the field where she had played soccer for so many years. She had been the goalie on a championship team. She remembered how angry she would get at herself when she allowed someone on the opposing team to score.

She looked inside the gym and the field house that had a swimming pool. She had been on the swim team most of her upper school years. She missed those carefree days when she was in school. She wished she could turn back the clock, but she knew that was impossible and so she was left with the memories.

She remembered walking through the park with her father. She could even hear the words of wisdom that he often shared with her.

“When you learn enough to really live, princess, then you're old enough to die.” He had always called her princess. “Oh, Dad. I wish you were here now,” she said to herself. She wished they could have another father daughter talk. She would love some advice on how to live and love in today's world.

Ingrid's thoughts turned to John. He should be arriving home about now she thought. She tried to imagine what he would be doing. She pictured the snow topped mountains that she had seen in books. "I wish I could be there with him," she thought as she walked toward home.

After a few days, it was time for Ingrid to leave for Findel Airport northeast of Luxembourg City. She would leave her car for her mother to use while she was gone. Her mother drove her to the airport very slowly. Ingrid hugged her mother for a long time before going through security at the airport. She saw a tear in her mother's eye as she left the security area. Leaving this beautiful country to go to a country so full of danger required a huge amount of faith. As much as Ingrid loved her work, she had a lot of apprehension.

The plane left for Brussels, and from there it would go on to Tel Aviv. As she settled back in her window seat, she thought again about some words her father had said to her about faith. "Faith," he would say, "is reaching out into the unknown and getting hold of that which is not and holding on until it becomes that which is." Well, she thought, I'm sure reaching out into the unknown this time. "Oh, God," she whispered, "please help me strengthen my faith. I know I will need Your help to do this job and to stay safe."

The flight to Tel Aviv was uneventful. When the plane landed and taxied into one of the most security-conscious terminals in the world, Ingrid's stomach began to churn. What am I doing here, she wondered? God, I sure hope I am in Your will. She glanced out of the window and saw a man standing by a van urinating. Not much modesty here she thought. Not much different than most of Europe.

When she left the plane, she got into a long line to go through security and customs. She quickly realized that it would not be a fast process. The officials took adequate time to ensure that each person represented no threat to the nation of Israel.

After a long interrogation, Ingrid was granted access into Israel. She retrieved her luggage, walked outside, and caught a cab to Jerusalem. She looked out the window as they drove, realizing even more the vast difference of this country. The terrain was rough and rocky. She saw burned out and damaged military vehicles abandoned by the sides of the road and in fields. The houses built on the sides of the hills were in small communities. There was evidence of hostility everywhere she looked. They frequently passed military jeeps filled with young men and women. The young citizens of Israel were required to serve in the military before they could go to college or begin a career. She felt a pain of loneliness and homesickness roll over her, and suddenly she missed John so much. She wished he could be here with her.

She checked into the King David Hotel, unpacked, ate dinner, and went to bed, quickly falling asleep. She dreamed of walking the streets of Bruges with John and riding a boat through the beautiful city. When she woke up and realized it was only a dream, she cried.

CHAPTER 4 - JOHN

John had dozed off at his desk when he heard someone calling his name. "John, John, earth to John," his secretary was calling his name. He ran his fingers through his hair as he answered her. "I'm sorry. I guess I dozed off," he said.

"I finished your PowerPoint presentation. Would you like to review it?" she asked.

"Yes, I need to make sure I don't forget anything."

Life had not been the same for him since he returned from Belgium. He was having a hard time keeping his mind on his work. He found himself thinking about Ingrid and missing her more than he ever thought he could miss anyone. He looked at his watch and estimated that she must be in Israel by now. He would wait until later to call her. He thought she would need time to rest after she arrived.

He wished he'd had more time with her before he left – more time to strengthen their relationship. He intended to be more intimate in his next phone conversation with her.

He knew in his heart that this was the most special relationship that he had ever experienced. He could not understand why he had trouble finding the right words to tell her just how he felt. Maybe he was afraid of rejection. Rejection was so painful, and he didn't want to experience it ever again. Once was enough in any person's life, he thought. I will never forget Katherine; I wish things would have been different.

He stood up and walked over to the window to look at the snow-covered mountain peaks. This view always inspired him. God sure knew what he was doing when he created these mountains. John's secretary came to the door. "Do you need anything else?" she asked.

"No thanks. Take off, and I'll see you tomorrow," he replied.

In a couple of days, he would be on his way to the airport again. This time he would go to visit a client in Mexico City. John realized that he would have to pull himself together because this client created a challenging interaction. He wanted to talk to Ingrid before he began this trip.

He calculated the time difference and knew she would probably be awake, so he called her cell phone. His heart pounded when he heard her voice. They had a long heart-to-heart conversation and shared their intimate feelings. The conversation ended with "I love you" on both ends. He felt better and more ready for his trip after talking to her.

On Sunday morning, John boarded a flight for Mexico City. It had been some time since he had been this far into Mexico. He had been in this client's other plants closer to the border, but he had never been to this location before. The plant manufactured parts for military helicopters.

John sat in a window seat in business class, so he had a good view as they approached the airport. The city was surrounded by mountain ranges, but the city itself was hard to see because of the surrounding smog. Not a very inviting view, he thought. Twenty-two million people lived or existed in this valley. He remembered reading about some beautiful cities in which to live and even retire to such as Guadalajara and San Miguel. But this city was not one that he would want to live in.

After landing, John walked into the area where he was supposed to meet his driver. The plant had arranged to have a driver pick him up. Finally, he saw a short man holding up a sign with his name on it. He waved at the man as they approached each other. "Señor Martin. My name is Pedro," he said. "Follow me, please." He took one of John's bags and pushed his way through the crowd toward the exit. "Be very careful, Señor Martin. There are many pickpockets. You can be robbed here in the airport if you are not careful."

"Thank you, Pedro. I will be careful." John said as he placed his hand over his wallet.

Once outside, they walked towards a large van. Pedro opened the back door and placed the luggage inside. He invited John to get in the front seat. Pedro got behind the wheel and started trying to maneuver his way in the traffic toward the hotel. After thirty minutes of heavy traffic, he pulled into the hotel. He helped John take his luggage inside and said, "I will pick you up at 7:30 am tomorrow morning. Have a good evening, Señor." John waved and said, "OK, see you early," as Pedro headed toward the van.

Once in his room, John unpacked and then went in search of a place to have dinner. A few doors down the street, he found the restaurant that the desk clerk had recommended. It was a lovely old seventeenth century building that had a lot of character. The aromas of chili and spices greeted him. Looking at the menu, he noticed some unusual items - fried baby worms and ant eggs in a special cream sauce. After some thought, he selected a more traditional Mexican dinner. The food was excellent.

Afterwards, John returned to his hotel room and dialed Ingrid's number. He lay across the bed while the phone rang. Soon, he heard a sleepy voice say,

"Hello."

"Hi, Ingrid. It's John."

"John, I am so glad you called. I've been thinking about you. I hope your trip to Mexico went well," she said.

"Yes, I am here, and the trip was smooth. I just miss you so much. I've been trying to figure out when we can get together again, but I'm at a loss. You seem so far away."

"I know," she said. "I have been having the same thoughts. Somehow, we will find a way. I don't know when or how, but I know we will."

"I'll give it more thought. I've always wanted to visit Israel. Now I have a good reason," he said with a smile in his voice. They talked for a few more minutes before saying goodnight.

John went to his briefcase, pulled out a photograph of Ingrid that she had given him on their last night together, set it beside his bed, and crawled in. She would be the last sight he saw before going to sleep and the first one when he woke up. He went to sleep thinking about her. The next morning, he was up and waiting before Pedro arrived to take him to the plant.

Bob Madison, the plant manager, was from Fort Worth, Texas. He had overseen the Dallas division before coming to Mexico City. He told John he had been in Mexico City for three years as they walked out of his office to begin touring the plant.

They walked through the facility and looked at the production process. It was apparent to John right away that things were very different here than in the U.S. Mexico did not have the strict OSHA and EPA laws like the U.S. Workers here were treated poorly and not protected, much like many other third-world countries. John saw a worker on a wooden ladder forty feet in the air without any type of fall protection. If the man were to fall, he would be seriously injured or killed. If that should happen, he would simply be replaced with another worker. There was little that could be done to protect workers because the government was unwilling to enforce any type of worker protection laws. "Bribery and kickbacks are a way of life here," Bob said.

Bob and John gathered in a small conference room with the senior staff. John had agreed to begin developing a strategic plan that would guide them through the next three years. The plan would enable them to focus on key business goals and improve production and profits, while at the same time implementing some safety guides.

On Friday morning, John arrived at the plant early hoping to finish work and leave for the airport by noon. Bob and John reviewed the key points the managers should focus on when Bob's secretary stepped into the room. "I'm sorry, Señor, but there is an urgent phone call for Mr. Madison," she said.

"Excuse me, John," this must seem terribly important for her to interrupt.

"No problem, Bob," John replied.

Bob suddenly yelled, "No! No! No!" and slammed the phone down. Bob said to John, "Let's go. I'll explain in the car."

As they were running out the door, Bob told his secretary to have the driver bring the car to the front immediately and call corporate security in Dallas and patch them through to his cell phone.

As they jumped in the car, John asked, "What's going on?" "Bandits have taken my wife hostage," he replied. "This sort of thing happens all too often here. Bandits kidnap foreign executives or their family members and hold them for ransom. Apparently, bandits broke into my home this morning soon after I left and kidnapped my wife. A neighbor heard Jane screaming as she was dragged out the front door and thrown into a van."

"I'm so sorry. What can I do to help?" John asked.

"I don't know what we are up against yet, just say lots of prayers if you are a praying man," Bob requested.

"I do believe in prayer, and I will do that," John replied.

When they arrived at Bob's house, the local police were there asking questions of bystanders. Bob rushed up to the officer that appeared to be in charge. "I'm her husband. What do you know so far, and what are you doing to find her?" Bob asked in a rush of words and emotion.

The officer replied in a nonchalant manner, "Señor, calm down. We are in charge here, and we know what we are doing. We are gathering information."

Bob grabbed him by the collar yelling, "Are you looking for my wife?"

The officer paused, looked around, removed Bob's hands, and pulled him aside. "We will begin looking, but you need to understand how these things work. The kidnappers are long gone and hidden away by now," he said.

Bob put his face in his hands and sobbed. John walked over to Bob, put an arm around his shoulders, and led him into the house. "Bob, you must sit down, and try to pull yourself together."

"You don't understand. The police are often in on kidnappings, and they get a nice piece of the action for stalling and giving the bandits time to get away," Bob responded.

Bob's phone rang. His secretary put the call through from corporate security. "Several top security people are on their way here already. They're accustomed to handling this kind of crisis," Bob said as though he were trying to reassure himself.

Nearly an hour had passed, and there had been no news. The house phone suddenly rang. Bob grabbed one phone and the police officer grabbed another phone. "We have your wife," said a gravelly voice. "We will not harm her if you pay us five hundred thousand American dollars."

Bob quickly asked, "Is she OK? Have you harmed her? Let me talk to her, or you get nothing."

"You can talk to her after you deliver the money," the man said firmly. "You have twenty-four hours to deliver it, or we will kill her," the man said.

The phone line went dead and the policeman hung up and looked at the two of them. "I'm sure that was not long enough for us to trace the call," Bob said with a long sigh.

About twenty minutes later the corporate security team arrived. Bob's phone rang, and he talked to his boss in Dallas. "We'll dispatch the money right away," he said as he tried to reassure Bob. "Our security team will know how to handle things. Please try to trust them. We have you and Jane in our prayers."

“Thanks,” Bob replied and hung up.

“I should have left my wife in Texas,” he said partially to me but mostly to himself. “I knew the dangers here. I should have left Jane in Dallas,” he continued.

John stood by silently praying, not really knowing what to do or say. So, he listened. He was shocked by the events of the day and decided to call the airport and extend his return flight home until Sunday. He couldn’t leave here and leave Bob to deal with this crisis alone. He wanted to stay with Bob and pray for him and Jane.

“Thanks, John. I appreciate you staying,” Bob said. The security team from the U.S. had taken over working with the Mexican police, which gave Bob some peace of mind.

A couple of hours later, the chief security officer, Frank Kilpatrick, walked over to Bob shaking his head. “Can you believe these thugs?” he said. “The local police chief said he would bring us the head of the bandit leader in a sack for $50,000. He obviously knows who they are and is in on the plot,” Frank said.

“I'm not surprised,” Bob responded. “The police are bandits themselves. They could bring the head of anyone, and we wouldn't know the difference,” Bob continued.

Frank talked briefly about the difficulties they always encountered when working with Mexican authorities. “Most of them are part of the organized crime in this country, primarily run by drug dealers. They kidnap to supplement their income from drugs and other crimes. Kidnapping has been on the rise in the last few years. The government recently fired over 3,000 police officers who were linked to criminal activities and for failing to do their jobs.

John listened as they continued talking. “Dear God,” he prayed, “we live in such a corrupt world. We sure do need your help, guidance, and protection.”

Around midnight, the security team finally convinced Bob to try to get some rest. John lay on the sofa drifting in and out of sleep. Bob got up before daybreak and showered and dressed, too anxious about Jane to rest.

John had the driver take him back to the hotel. He had left his luggage at the front desk, planning to pick it up on his way to the airport. He got another room, slept a few hours before getting showered and dressed, and went back to Bob’s house.

Shortly before noon on Saturday, another security team arrived from the U.S. with the ransom money. Arrangements had been made to drop it off and make an exchange for Jane. They would have to take a risk and leave the ransom money before getting her. They knew it could backfire, but the kidnappers left them no choice. They dropped the ransom money at an abandoned warehouse, then went several blocks away to an old car sitting on blocks beside the road to collect Jane. Miraculously, Jane was found bound and gagged in the trunk. She was shaken and scared but otherwise unharmed.

Frank, head of the security team, led the way to the hospital where Jane would be checked out. On the way, he placed a call to Bob. “We have her. She seems to be OK. Meet us at the hospital,” he said.

“Oh, thank God! I'm on the way. Thanks, Frank. I appreciate all you've done,” Bob said.

Bob and John ran out the door, jumped in the van, and the driver sped toward the hospital. “Thank you, God,” John whispered as they raced toward the hospital. Bob grabbed John's shoulder and shook his hand. “Thanks for staying with me. I appreciate your support and prayers.”

“You're welcome. I'm so thankful that you have her back and that she's OK.”

“Jane and I will leave on the company plane with the security team as soon as she is released from the hospital. My driver will take care of you and make sure you get to the airport,” Bob said.

“Thanks, Bob. I'll be in touch in a few days to check on you and Jane. I'll be back in Denver next week if you need anything.”

They parted at the hospital. Since it was late, the driver took John back to the hotel. “I will be here at 8:00 am to take you to the airport, Señor.”

“I'll be ready,” John replied.

The trip to the airport was slow, even for a Sunday morning. The traffic was always horrible in Mexico City. John thought, Now I know what had happened to all the old-style VW bugs when they were no longer available in the U.S. They're all here - as green and white taxi cabs.

They finally arrived at the airport. “Goodbye, Pedro,” John said as he checked his luggage in at the Delta counter.

“See you next time, Señor,” Pedro said as he started back to the parking lot.

John struggled through the line boarding the plane. He lifted his heavy case into the overhead storage bin and fell into his seat with a sigh. What people have to go through to make a living, he thought. Every day he was becoming more aware of how violent this world is. Executives and their families were in danger in so many countries. There was so much poverty in many countries that people would do almost anything to get a little money. In many countries, such as Africa, he realized that they were never caught or brought to justice, primarily because everyone was afraid to look for them.

For the next few months, things were routine and uneventful. Bob called and reported that Jane was now living in Dallas, and he was commuting to Mexico City each week. They scheduled a follow-up meeting for three months later.

John's next visit to Belgium was very tough since Ingrid was not there. He walked where they had walked with a great sadness in his heart. They talked weekly and emailed almost daily, but it was not the same.

"Time flies like an arrow," someone once said. John realized that as time flies, so our lives fly by all too fast. He remembered a poem by an unknown author that he had read a long time ago:

First, I was dying to finish high school and start college.

And then I was dying to finish college and start working.

And then I was dying to marry and have children.

And then I was dying to retire.

And now I am dying.

And suddenly I realize I forgot to live.

John thought that he felt more alive now than he had in a long time, but for years he had forgotten to really live and focus on what is most important. A friend that he met when he was a young man once told him, "John, when you learn enough to really live, you will be old enough to die." Well maybe he had been a slow learner, but he'd sure had a lot of hard lessons in life.

The most painful experience occurred about seven years ago. It still hurt to think about it, so most of the time he tried not to think about Katherine. They were engaged to be married after dating for two years. He was so excited at the thought of having a life with this beautiful woman. They had so much fun together and enjoyed traveling and experiencing new places and things. They often took weekend flights to various cities where they would simply walk and hold hands. They traveled from the east coast to the west coast.

The things they had enjoyed were so simple, yet they were so enjoyable. They would rent a car in San Francisco and drive up Highway 1 to Stinson's Beach and have breakfast. They would talk for hours and never get tired of each other's company.

They had made plans to build a home and have children. They wanted a log home in the mountains where their children could grow up and be surrounded by nature and pets. A few months before their wedding day, John got a phone call that shook his world. "John," Katherine said, "I don't feel right. I'm dizzy and lightheaded, and I have a terrible headache. John rushed to pick her up and take her to the doctor. When he arrived, she wasn't home. Her mother had already taken her to the doctor, who had immediately rushed her to the hospital. Gripped by fear, John rushed to the hospital to be by her side. After two days of extensive tests, the doctor called the family and John into his office to talk. The doctor sat behind his desk with a worried look on his face. "I hate having to tell you, but the news is not good," he began. "Katherine has a brain tumor. We don't know if it's malignant yet, but we feel the best course of treatment at this stage is to operate. We need to try to get it out. The tumor is large, and we might not be able to remove all of it. We won't know until we get a closer look at it."

Katherine's mother began to cry softly. John sat with his head in his hands, unable to speak because of the lump in his throat.

Several minutes later, they walked out of the doctor's office in a daze. John walked slowly down the hall to the elevators. Katherine's parents decided to go to the chapel to pray. John took the elevator to Katherine's floor and walked slowly to her room. He stood outside for a few minutes, then walked in.

She was awake and looking out the window. Her eyes were red from crying. John walked over, grasped her hand, and kissed her softly. He sat down on the edge of her bed and tears started to flow down his cheeks. He was still unable to speak. He couldn't think of words that seemed appropriate.

"John, it's OK," Katherine whispered. "I will be alright."

"I know," he was finally able to speak.

"John, listen to me. If I don't make it, I want you to go on with your life. Find someone and have a good life. That is what I want," she said.

"Katherine, how could I live without you?" he replied. "I want you to make it. I need you, and I love you dearly," John said between sobs.

John spent the night at the hospital holding

Katherine's hand and talking with her about their plans for their home and their life together. He encouraged her to sleep. He knew she would need lots of rest in the coming days, but she insisted on staying awake and talking. "I don't want to waste a moment with you," she whispered.

Early the next morning, preparations were made for surgery. John kissed Katherine and left the room when her parents arrived. He knew they needed time alone with her. He went to the chapel and prayed until Katherine's father came to get him. "They'll take her in a few moments. I know you want to be there. Please join us," he said.

The surgery lasted for several hours. Dr. Johnson, the surgeon, came to see the family when it was over. "She is stable for now," he said. "However, we were not able to get the entire tumor. It was a very complicated surgery, and we did the best we could. This means that she will need additional treatment. I will be meeting with a team of oncologists to discuss her treatment. We will meet with you once we have developed a plan. I'm so sorry I don't have better news," he said and then turned and walked away.

They stood motionless for some time. Katherine's mother started to cry; her husband took her in his arms and walked out of the room with her. John walked to the window and stared at nothing. "Dear God," he whispered, "what do we do now?"

Katherine was taken to ICU after the surgery, so the amount of time they could spend with her was very limited. When John walked into her room, he viewed a sea of machines and cables attached to her. She opened her eyes when he grasped her hand and kissed her on the forehead. She gave him a faint smile and squeezed his hand. He told her how much he loved her and that she was going to be OK. The 10 minutes flew by, and he had to leave the room. He kissed her again before leaving.

Katherine's mother decided to take her back to their home in Dallas to recover. Katherine was too weak to protest, and John had to travel for work so he couldn't be there to look after her needs. Katherine's mother became extremely protective, and Katherine became her focus. As Katherine regained some of her strength she started painting again, something she had always enjoyed doing.

Her mother enjoyed having Katherine at home and began to resist the plan that Katherine would move back to Denver and get married. During the next few months as Katherine underwent chemotherapy, her mother moved Katherine to Arizona without telling anyone. She intercepted phone calls and said that Katherine was not available. She wouldn't give Katherine messages, and she changed their number to unlisted so that John had no way of contacting them.

After searching for months with no luck, John had to accept that he had no choice but let go of Katherine. He had to try to move on with his life. Three years went by and he received a phone call from Katherine's mother telling him that Katherine had passed away a few months earlier. She begged him to forgive her for shutting him out of Katherine's life. She told him that Katherine never stopped loving him and talked about him until the end. After the call, John doubled over with grief and spent the next few days at home grieving for Katherine. For the first time, he had given himself permission to grieve for her. Since John had captured her mother's phone number on his caller I.D., he called her and found out where Katherine was buried.

Two days later, he boarded a plane for Tucson, rented a car and drove to the cemetery where Katherine was buried. He placed flowers on her grave and cried for a long time. He said all the things he wanted to say to her before and hoped that she could hear him from heaven.

It was difficult for him not to feel bitter towards Katherine's mother, and he had prayed for strength to forgive her. It was difficult knowing that Katherine's mother had placed her own needs above Katherine's needs. When Katherine died, a part of him died with her. He had not allowed himself to love again until he met Ingrid.

John followed Fox news each day, and he was concerned as tension in Israel was obviously growing. Iran was now threatening to wipe Israel off the map with the nuclear weapons they were developing. Each day, he prayed for Ingrid's safety. And each day, he had to trust God to take care of her in one of the most hostile places in the world.

CHAPTER 5 – INGRID & DAVID

Ingrid struggled in her heart and mind over her move to Jerusalem. It was a wonderful city, but she found it impossible to feel happy in one of the most interesting places in the world. When she arrived from Tel Aviv, she had checked into the King David Hotel and placed a call to her boss at Fox to let him know she had arrived. He informed her that David Friedman, her cameraman, would be contacting her the next morning. David would show her around and help her find a place to live and get settled. "You can trust David," he informed her. "He has worked for us for a long time and has proven himself to be trustworthy."

The next morning after getting dressed, Ingrid got a call from the front desk. "Mr. Friedman is waiting for you in the coffee shop," the voice on the phone informed her.

When she walked into the coffee shop, she saw a tall, slim man sitting at a table sipping coffee. "Shalom," he said as she approached. "You must be Ingrid," he said smiling. "I'm David. Welcome to Jerusalem."

"Shalom," she replied. "It's nice to meet you," she said as she extended her hand for a handshake. After a cup of coffee, David said, "I will show you our beautiful city. We will begin by visiting the old walled city of Jerusalem."

They drove from the Mount of Olives and up the hill to the walled city. After parking in a lot near the Jaffa Gate, they entered the city. "This is the largest city in Israel, and it is the capitol. Inside, the city walls the area is about 220 acres. The current walls were built by

Suleiman the Magnificent in the 16th century. The gates of the city were angled so that invaders could not use battering rams and charge into the city at full gallop on horseback. They would have to make a ninety degree turn which would slow them down," David pointed out.

Ingrid was speechless as she walked through the ancient city. "I have always wanted to see this place," she said. She was amazed at the variety of shops and vendors selling all types of souvenirs, spices, and fruits.

They walked through the Armenian Quarter and saw people going about their daily activities. As they walked through the Jewish Quarter and then past the Wailing Wall, they saw people stuffing pieces of paper containing prayer requests into the cracks in the wall. They walked through the Muslim Quarter where they found Arab markets. Ingrid bought a pastry from a vendor with a green cart full of bagels and a variety of pastries.

David informed Ingrid that if she wanted to see the area around the Dome of The Rock, they must be there early in the morning. "They only allow access to non-Muslims at certain times," he pointed out. "Years ago, you could walk through anytime, but not anymore. Security is very tight. There are even gun ports on the sides of the temple walls."

They continued their tour and walked through the Christian Quarter. Ingrid asked David many questions, which he patiently answered. David told her, "At night, they conduct tours underground along the Western Wall, and you can see the original foundation that King Solomon built and touch the rock of the mountain where Abraham came to offer his son Isaac as a sacrifice before God stopped him and provided a ram for the sacrifice."

"Please. I want to do that tour very soon," Ingrid replied.

"OK. I will make the necessary reservations," he said.

After a few hours of sightseeing, they walked back out the Jaffa Gate. "Wow! What an incredible place!" stated Ingrid.

"There is no place in the world like this place" David responded.

"I can hardly believe that I'm really here and that this will be my home for some time," she said.

David continued, "There is a line from the movie **RAIDERS OF THE LOST ARK** about this place. Indiana Jones threatens to blow up the Ark of the Covenant. His nemesis pats the Ark and says, **"You and I are just passing through history. This is history.** "

"Yes," she agreed, "Jerusalem is definitely history. We've just walked through a large part of history."

As they drove back to towards the hotel, Ingrid said, "David, tell me a little about you,"

He began by saying, "I was born and educated in Israel. I am married to a wonderful woman who works for the Israeli government as a research scientist. Much of her work is top secret, so I don't know much about what she is researching. We have been married for eight years, and we have two children – ages three and five. I have been with Fox News for three years. Our last correspondent was killed by an explosion on her bus. She was not killed immediately but died a few days after the bombing."

He continued, “We are glad Fox found a replacement so quickly. It usually takes a long time to get a replacement. Many people are too afraid to come here.”

“Well,” she responded, “I had requested a transfer but didn’t know when it would come through. I'm not married, so I was able to move quickly.”

"Everyone at Fox in Jerusalem is glad that you were able to arrive so quickly. We will make every effort to teach you how to remain safe here. There are many things we will show you and teach you in the next few days that will help you remain safe while you are living and working in this Holy City. As you know, there is a lot of violence here. Hamas is very active in this part of the world, and you must constantly be aware of your surroundings. When you enter restaurants, you will notice that there are guards inspecting backpacks and purses. They are looking for bombs.”

“Tomorrow I will show you your apartment,” David continued. “Fox has selected a place for you in an area that is safer than most areas. I will pick you up at 8:00 tomorrow morning, and we will go there."

“OK” she replied as she got out of the van. “I'll see you then.”

After dinner in the hotel restaurant, Ingrid went to bed early. She was feeling the effects of jet lag and the time change. She went to sleep thinking about John and wishing that they were closer.

Ingrid was awakened around 3:00 am by a loud noise outside her hotel. She fumbled around in the dark to find her cell phone which was ringing.

Expecting to hear John's voice, she was disappointed to hear David saying, "Get dressed. There has been a bombing in a hotel near you. I will pick you up in twenty minutes."

"OK. I'll be ready," she mumbled as she headed to the bathroom. She was accustomed to having to rush to incidents and normally had clothing and everything out so she could get ready quickly. However, with most of her belongings still in her luggage, it took a little longer.

She met David in the lobby, and they hurried out the door. "It's only a few blocks away. It will be better if we walk," he stated.

"Sure thing," she said as she hurried along.

David was carrying his camera and sound equipment and was obviously ready to go to work. Rounding the corner, they could see the chaos and a crowd assembled in front of one of the hotels that Americans often used. Police had taped off an area around the hotel and would not allow reporters to get close to the lobby area.

"They are afraid that there will be a second bomb," David said. "Often a second bomb is set by the terrorist hoping to kill more people after a crowd gathers at the site," he concluded.

Ingrid stood in front of the hotel and reported while David filmed. "Good morning, this is Ingrid Bauer reporting live from Jerusalem. It is quite early in the morning here, and a bomb has just gone off at the Marriott hotel. It is feared that many are dead and wounded. We have been informed that the hotel was fully occupied by American tour groups. No one has yet claimed responsibility for the bombing," she was saying, "but Hamas or the Taliban is suspected. We will continue to give you live updates as more information is available."

They watched in silence as ambulances carried away the dead and wounded victims of the attack. David continued to film the activities, but both were speechless except when they conducted a live update.

They were at the scene for several hours giving updates as more information became available. By the time they left, they were both exhausted and hungry. They walked back toward Ingrid's hotel, found a restaurant, and had a late lunch. "We'll wait until tomorrow to get you to your apartment if that is OK with you," David said.

"That is fine with me. I am so tired, and my feet are killing me," she replied.

"You don't have to wear heels to report from here, I will just do upper body shots," he said.

"Thanks," she replied, "I think I will go take a nap. Call me if anything else happens" she said.

CHAPTER 6 - JOHN

John had been working in London. His hotel phone rang with a British voice saying, "Good morning, Mr. Martin. This is your wake-up call." It was 6:00 am in London. He stumbled out of bed and turned on the TV. He had a habit of watching Fox now for obvious reasons. He was shaving when he heard a voice that he recognized. Rushing to the TV, he saw Ingrid. She was reporting from Jerusalem about a hotel bombing in the city. It was so good to hear her voice and know that she was OK. He decided to give her a quick call before heading off to work. His heart leaped when she answered. "Oh, John! I'm so glad you called. What a terrible night," she said.

"I saw your report on Fox News a few minutes ago. Are you alright?" he asked.

"Yes, I'm fine. Just tired. But it's so good to hear your voice."

"I miss you so much," he said, "We must find a way to see each other soon." After a short conversation, they planned to meet in Belgium in two weeks for the weekend. John rushed off to work. The rest of the day, John ached inside, missing her and being concerned for her safety in such a dangerous part of the world. I wish I could be there with her, he thought. I love her so much.

The following week, John was having dinner with a client in California onboard the Queen Mary that was dry docked in Long Beach. John was enjoying the view when his cell phone rang.

"Excuse me. I'm expecting a call from my

secretary," John said as he stepped away. "Hello, this is John."

"John, it's Ingrid."

"Hello, Ingrid. I'm so glad you called. Are you OK?"

"Yes, but I don't have much time, and I have something important to tell you. I'm being sent on an assignment to Jordan for several days. I'm not sure how long, but it seems to be something urgent and maybe a little dangerous. I just wanted to let you know. I won't be able to meet you in Belgium as we'd planned."

"I'm sorry to hear that. I was looking forward to seeing you, but I understand. Please be careful. Will you be able to phone me from there?" John asked.

"I'm not sure, but I'll certainly try to," she replied. Ingrid continued to apologize, "John, I am so sorry. I don't have much choice. I miss you, John, and I love you," she said.

"I miss you too, and I love you very much. I'll be praying for you and your safety."

They said goodbye. After taking a moment to gather himself, John walked back to the table and sat down, visibly upset.

After finishing dinner, John drove back to his hotel and walked wearily to his room. He lay across his bed and started to pray. "Dear God, he whispered, please take care of the woman I love." After praying for a long time, he finally fell asleep. He woke up the next morning when the clock went off and realized that he had not even undressed.

As he showered and shaved, he kept thinking about Ingrid saying she loved him and how wonderful it was to feel loved. He tried calling her to tell her again how much she meant to him but got her voicemail. He left her a message and hung up.

She may already be on a plane to Amman, he thought. If so, she probably had to fly from Israel to someplace in Europe and then back to Amman. It was unlikely that she could fly directly from Israel to Jordan or any other Arab country.

John realized that their relationship had risen to a new level now that they were deeply in love with each other. In the beginning, it had been a wonderful, flirtatious activity with lots of uncertainty. Now it was a serious relationship with a lot of hopes and dreams for a life together. It was something good, with potential for a future that would involve commitment. He thought about the meaning of love he had once heard - love is an unconditional commitment to an imperfect person. Well he thought to himself, I am certainly an imperfect person. He thought about the old saying that love is blind. To John, it seemed more accurate to say that love is based on mutual needs and desires. When a man has the desire to meet a woman's needs, and when a woman has the desire to meet a man's needs, then it seemed like a win-win love. Love is an act of the will, and love is an action, not just words. Time would tell how much action there would be in this relationship. John wondered how a woman who seemed as perfect as Ingrid could possibly love him. "Well, God, I don't know all of the answers, but I thank you that she does love me. I am certainly blessed."

Over the next several days, John tried calling Ingrid but had no luck reaching her. He listened to the news each evening hoping for a clue about what she was working on and whether or not she was safe. But there was nothing in the news about Jordan. He also searched the internet, but again found no clues. All he could do was pray for her safety.

John had no other way of getting information since he didn't know her family or how to reach them. He realized that there was so much about her that he didn't know. He also realized that she probably had not had an opportunity to contact her family since finding out that she had to go to Jordan.

CHAPTER 7 - DAVID & INGRID

David picked Ingrid up at her apartment, and they headed for the airport. "Ingrid, I am so sorry that I have to take you to Jordan. I'm not sure why we're going. All I know is that we're supposed to investigate what is happening in Petra," he said.

"I know David. We have a job to do, and we'll give it our best effort," she replied.

"I've checked with my contacts in the Israeli Army and have learned nothing. There are some underground contacts that think there's terrorist activity going on in Petra. The terrorists are conducting bombing activities in various areas, and possibly are the ones who bombed the Marriott hotel," he said. "There is also a rumor that the Jordanian government has closed Petra to tourists. This would be unheard of since they are so dependent upon tourist trade. If it is closed, there must be another source of income. Otherwise, the area would have nothing. That source could be money from terrorist organizations. I suspect that might be the reason we're being sent to investigate. If it's true, it will be very dangerous," he concluded.

"Tell me more about Petra," said Ingrid.

"Well it's an ancient city that was carved out of stone inside the mountain. It has been used by different groups as a natural fortress for hundreds of years. There is only one entrance to the interior of the city. It is through a narrow passageway that is almost one mile long," he responded.

"Wow, it sounds like a tough assignment," she said.

"You're right about that. No matter what we find, it will not be easy, and it will certainly involve risk. You must be careful at all times," he said again.

David and Ingrid landed in Amman just before midnight and took a taxi to the hotel on the side of a hill giving a good view of the city down below. Ingrid walked out on the balcony and thought about John as she looked at the lights below. She realized that she loved him more than she thought possible. She investigated the starry night and whispered a prayer before going inside and trying to sleep.

At daybreak, Ingrid woke up and got dressed. She and David had planned to meet in the in the hotel dining area for breakfast at 7:00. Breakfast consisted of breads, cheeses, smoked salmon, ham, and fruits. The smell of freshly baked bread drew David and Ingrid like magnets. When they sat down, they were so hungry that few words were exchanged.

After a while, they talked about what they needed to do to get started. David had wanted to call his wife and family the night before, but it was too late, so he took a few minutes to call them.

"My cell phone isn't working here," Ingrid said.

"When we get back to Israel, we'll get you a phone that will work here. The cell phones are different here. Even though your phone works in Israel, it won't work in other middle eastern countries," he said. "We could get you one here, but there are very few towers in Jordan, and it is unlikely that it would work outside of Amman. We'll be driving several hours into remote parts of Jordan. You're welcome to use my phone while we're here," he said.

"Thanks. If you don't mind, I would like to make a quick call," she said. He handed her the phone and went to refill his coffee. Ingrid dialed John's number but got his voicemail. She knew that when he was conducting workshops, he turned his phone off. She left a short message and told him she loved and missed him.

Ingrid tossed her bag over her shoulder and said to David, "I'll get my luggage and meet you in the lobby in fifteen minutes."

"OK. I'll pick up the rental. It was dropped off here a few minutes ago," David said.

Soon they were bouncing along the roads of Jordan headed for Petra. "I'm amazed at the contrast in the desert here compared to the desert in Israel," said Ingrid. "In Israel the desert blooms like a rose. There are so many groves of fig trees and places where flowers grow. It is so beautiful. Here it is barren with little vegetation of any kind," she remarked.

"Yes," said David, "In Israel, they have irrigated the desert, draining water from the Jordan River. Here it is like it has been for thousands of years." He continued, "As a result, you will see much poverty here. People have little to do so they live in poverty even in the towns and villages."

"Where is Petra?" asked Ingrid.

"Several hours drive from here" he replied. "It is quite a place," he remarked. "Petra is known as the lost city in Southern Jordan. It is a city carved out of rock and hidden inside a large mountain range with a narrow passageway. The entrance is so narrow that only a very small vehicle can pass through, and people normally ride in on mules and horses or they walk."

"David, if Hamas or Al Qaeda terrorists have taken control of Petra, what could they possibly do there that they can't do someplace else?" Ingrid inquired.

"I'm not sure, but hopefully that is a question we will be able to answer. I'm guessing that it provides privacy that other places don't provide. They can guard the entrance and feel safe. They can hide in the rooms carved in the rock, and no one can see what they're doing," he continued. "It's probably one of the most secure locations in the world for terrorists," said David.

His voice trailed off and he gazed out the windshield. They didn't talk much for the next fifty miles. They were both lost in thought about what they might find when they arrived in Petra. They wondered about the dangers, and they both silently prayed for their families and their loved ones. Ingrid wanted to talk to John, "Oh, God," she prayed "Please take care of him and make a way for us to be together again soon."

After what seemed like many hours, they arrived in the town built on the hillside above Petra. David remarked in a low voice, "This sure is a desolate place. I hope this investigation won't take too long."

"Me, too," Ingrid whispered.

They drove through town until they found a hotel that looked like it might be safe and checked in. The front desk clerk had a name tag on that indicated his name was Raul. David tried to speak to him in Hebrew and only got a stern look. He then tried speaking to him in English, and Raul seemed to understand. "We need two rooms," David said. Raul had them sign in and took their credit cards.

"How long will you be staying?" Raul inquired.

"We're not sure yet," David responded. Raul looked puzzled, "Then why are you here?" he inquired. "We're tourists traveling through this area and photographing the sights to sell to magazines," David said. That seemed to satisfy Raul's curiosity for now, and he handed them the keys to their rooms. David wasn't sure that Raul believed him, but he couldn't think of a better excuse now. He hadn't thought ahead of time what he should say if anyone asked him that question. He would certainly think it through now in case someone else asked him why they were there.

As they got on the elevator, they noticed that Raul was making a phone call and watching them intently.

"I wonder who he's calling," David said as the elevator door closed.

"I don't know, but his gaze sure makes me nervous," Ingrid said.

They went to their rooms after agreeing to meet in the lobby at 6:00 pm to find a place to have dinner. Ingrid was concerned about the security of the rooms. The only locks were flimsy push locks on the doorknobs and no deadbolts. She locked her door and headed into the bathroom to take a shower. Afterwards, she picked up her laptop and tried getting online, but with no luck. She tried her cell phone; it was useless also.

Since arriving in Israel, she had started keeping a journal on her laptop. She sat down at the little desk by the window and started recording the day's events. She also penned her thoughts about John and their life together. John, I miss you more than I can say. My heart aches when I think of you and how much I love you. I can hardly wait until we can be together again, she wrote.

The room was extremely hot, so she tried opening the window, hoping a breeze might flow through. The window opened slightly, but there was no breeze today. The average temperature for this area at this time of year was 108°F. Ingrid knew it would be difficult to adjust to the hot, dry weather. It was so different from Europe.

After finishing her journal entry, it was almost 6:00 pm, so she dressed and went down to meet David for dinner. He was waiting in the lobby, "Why don't we find out what restaurants are close by? I checked out the one here in the hotel and was not very impressed," he said.

"OK. That sounds good to me," she said. They asked the desk clerk, who pointed out a couple of places close by, so they decided to walk a few blocks and select one.

"I don't want to get too far away from the hotel," David said. "This is a dangerous country, and we really don't know what to expect. If there were more tourists here, I would feel more comfortable," he remarked. They found a small place around the corner from the hotel. They had lamb meatloaf with hummus, falafel, and pita bread. "This food is similar to the food in Israel," Ingrid said.

"Yes, much of the Middle East has food that is similar; yet some foods that are totally different," he replied.

The next morning, they met for coffee and the typical breakfast of cheese, lunch meats, and pastries. Ingrid recalled breakfasts when she attended training at Fox News in New York. No biscuits and gravy, or eggs and bacon, or sausage here. She wondered how John might like this breakfast. Then she calculated what time it was in Denver and what John might be doing today. "I really miss you, John," she whispered to herself.

"Did you say something?" David asked.

"I was just thinking out loud how much I miss John," she replied.

"I understand," David said. "I miss my wife and children so much, and who knows when I will see them again. I may never see them again," he said in a low voice.

"Don't allow yourself to think that way, David," she said. "We will do our best to look out for each other so that we make it home safe," she said.

After breakfast they drove down the narrow road to the bottom of the hill and the entrance of Petra. They were met by a military blockade. David was fluent in several Middle Eastern languages, so he did the talking. "Who is in charge here?" he asked.

A short, smelly guard carrying an AK 47 walked over to the window and asked, "What do you want?"

"We are here to take some photographs of Petra for a magazine," David replied.

"No one is allowed inside Petra," the guard said.

"Why can't we just take some photos for our magazine? We have driven a very long way," David said.

"No one is allowed inside Petra," the guard repeated in a very stern voice.

"We are willing to pay," David said, hoping the guard would accept a bribe. Instead, the guard pointed the end of the AK 47 at David and slowly shook his head no.

"Who are you?" the guard asked.

David pulled his Fox News identification out of his pocket and showed it to the guard. The guard looked at it and compared the photo on the ID to David. He handed it to another soldier who appeared to be in charge. He slowly looked at it and walked to the window of the vehicle.

"What are you doing here?" he asked.

"We just wanted to take some photos to sell to magazines," David answered.

"You lie," he said. "Why are you here"?

David, trying to keep the worry he felt inside from showing on his face, said, "I am not lying. We only want to take some pictures of this beautiful place in your country. My friend here has never seen Petra. You must agree with me that Petra is a beautiful place. Everyone should see it," David said.

"Yes," the guard responded, "but Petra is closed to all visitors, and no one can enter. I'm sorry for your long journey, but you must leave now," he said as he handed David his ID.

David slipped the car into reverse and slowly backed away. He turned around and headed back to the hotel. "Something is going on there," he said. "This place is a major tourist attraction, and many people will lose a lot of money if people cannot see it. It has never been guarded this heavily," David said as he pulled into the parking lot at the hotel.

After he parked, he took out his digital camera and his largest telephoto lens and started taking pictures of the entrance to Petra, especially the guards. "Are you sure it is OK to do that?" Ingrid asked.

"I'm hoping they didn't notice," said David as he finished and put the camera away.

As they he walked toward the hotel entrance, a military jeep pulled up and blocked their path. "Give us the camera," the guard demanded. "We told you no photographs, and we mean it," he said.

David went back to the vehicle, pulled out his old film camera, gave it to them, and closed the back. As they drove away, David chuckled, "There's nothing on that camera. It's blank. I used my other camera to take the picture – the digital one.

Back in the hotel, they sat down in the lobby with a cup of coffee and tried to figure out what the next step should be. "I'm not sure how to get into Petra now," David said. "There must be a way, but it will be dangerous with all those guards," he continued.

"Maybe we should just forget it and leave," Ingrid said.

"You might be right," said David. "However, this could be one of the biggest stories of the year, and we will be the ones that break it," he concluded. "Yes," she said, "but it could cost us our lives, and it would not be worth that," she said.

While they were discussing what to do, a man approached and sat down across from them. I am Omar. I want to help you with your mission here.

"What do you mean – our mission here?" David asked skeptically.

"I know you are not from here, so you must be on a mission to Petra. I can help get you into Petra," he said.

"How did you know we wanted to get into Petra?" David inquired.

"Sir, what would two people from Fox News be doing here if they didn't want to get into Petra? There's nothing else here of any interest."

"How do you know we are from Fox?" David asked with some anger in his voice.

"Too many questions. Do you want my help or not?" Omar inquired impatiently.

"How can you help us?" David asked.

"I know a way to get you into Petra. You will not be able to get inside without my help," he said.

David turned and looked at Ingrid, "What do you think?" he whispered to her.

"I don't know. Could we discuss it and talk to him in the morning?" she asked.

"Omar, could we meet you here in the morning and discuss your offer?" David asked.

"OK. I will meet you here at 8:00 am," he replied. With that he got up and walked away.

Ingrid looked at David and asked, "What should we do?"

He looked away and thought for a moment and sighed, "I'm really not sure. But if we don't get in there, we'll never get the real story about what is happening here. And we know for sure that something unusual is going on here. I think I should let him take me in and you stay at the hotel. That way, if something happens, at least you can let my family know what happened to me."

"I have to trust your judgment," she said, "but you better be sure that you get back because I wouldn't know how to get back to Amman. And I sure don't want to have to tell your wife that you are missing or hurt," she continued.

“I suppose it will depend on how much he's going to charge us to take me in. I'm sure he wants big bucks to do this. He's not doing it out of the goodness of his heart,” David said.

“I suppose we should meet with him in the morning and see what he charges and how he plans to do it,” she responded.

“I agree. Well, goodnight. I'm very tired,” David said.

“See you in the morning,” she said. With that they went to their rooms and tried to sleep. Sleep did not come easy in this kind of heat, but they finally dozed off. When they woke up the next morning neither of them felt rested; however, they showered and made their way down to the hotel restaurant for breakfast. They met in the lobby and found a table in the corner where they could see the entrance. Another buffet except there was not much on it, just coffee, pastry, and some cheese. “Not very tasty,” Ingrid remarked.

“You're right. This is a poor country, so the people don’t have very good food,” David responded.

They sat silently and ate for a few minutes, and then they saw Omar walk in. He came over to their table and pulled up a chair and sat down. “Good morning my friends,” he said as he rubbed his beard. “Have you thought about my offer to take you inside Petra?” he inquired.

“We have discussed it, but we need more information. Just how do you propose to get me in?” David asked.

“I will sneak you in on the wagon that goes inside each day carrying supplies,” he said.

“Why do they need daily supplies inside Petra?” David wanted to know.

"You will see for yourself when I take you inside," he said.

"Well let's talk about money," David said. "I don't think you are doing this out of the goodness of your heart."

"Ah, my friend, you come to the point, yes," Omar said as he leaned back in his chair and laughed. "You are right; I will take you inside for $1,000 U.S. dollars or $1200 Euros. I don't want Israeli money" he continued. "It is no good here."

David leaned back in his chair thoughtfully and slowly responded, "We will give you half when we leave and the other half when we get back."

Omar looked at him with a stern look, "I can see you do not trust me," he said.

"My motto has always been 'trust but verify.' I want to make sure I come out alive," David said.

"We will leave in 30 minutes," Omar said. "The wagon that goes inside leaves at 9:00 am. Get your equipment and meet me in the rear parking lot in 15 minutes," he continued.

As Omar walked out of the dining room, Ingrid looked at David. "Do you really want to do this? I don't feel good about it," she said.

"I have no choice. It's the only way to find out what is going on inside," he said.

"Where is Omar from?" she asked.

"I think he is a Bedouin. The tribes in this area dress like the way he is dressed. They wander like nomads and live in the desert in tents much like they have lived for hundreds of years," David answered. "The biggest difference is that today, they get around in pickup trucks instead of riding camels," he continued.

"Do you think he is trustworthy?" she asked.

"I doubt it, but I have little choice if we want to know why Petra is closed to the public," he replied. With that David pushed his chair back and headed up to his room to get the equipment he might need. He had gotten it together the night before in anticipation of the trip, so all he needed to do was pick up the cameras and backpack containing his laptop and sound equipment and leave for the parking lot.

Ingrid met him at the back door of the hotel. "Please be careful," she said as he walked out the door.

"I will. I hope to see you in a few hours," he said as he got into Omar's old minivan. Ingrid stood at the door for a long time wondering if she would ever see David again. She felt lost in this strange village without David. She said a prayer for his safety and walked over to the elevator and pushed the button for her floor. "Dear God," she prayed, "I am in a strange land with no way to communicate with others outside this country unless I can get my laptop to work on a satellite connection. Please help me get a connection."

She worked for a while trying to get a connection. When she finally got one, she sent an email to her boss, Joel Black, at Fox in New York telling him what was happening. She then sent an email to John, hoping he would get it and respond soon. She couldn't remember where he was working this week. She could only hope that he would be able to get the message and know where she was, and that she was still alive.

She lay down and eventually dozed off thinking about John and wishing she could hear his voice. She was awakened by a noise outside her door. It sounded like someone was outside her room. She slipped off the bed and started to walk toward the door as silently as she could. After a few steps she tripped over her backpack and stumbled. When she did, she knocked an ashtray off the end table. The glass breaking made a loud noise, but she also heard someone running down the hall. She raced to the door and opened it in time to see someone rounding the corner and running down the stairs.

As she walked back inside the room, she noticed that her foot was bleeding. She had obviously stepped on a piece of broken glass. The cut was not very deep, so she opened a small first aid kit she carried in her suitcase and took out a band aid. Then she sat down at the desk to check her email. She realized that she was frightened now. Why was someone waiting outside her room? How much danger was she in? What would she do if David didn't return soon? Questions flooded her mind.

On the way down the hill, David asked Omar what the plan was to get him inside. “It is simple,” he replied. "Each day, a small minivan goes inside with food and fresh water for the people who are working there. The passageway is very narrow and only a small vehicle can make it inside. I will put you inside the back of the van. When we get inside, I will take you to my comrade who will show you where to go so that you can get your photographs. After dark he will smuggle you out in the same minivan. At night, it brings all the trash outside, so the ride back will not be as pleasant,” he said.

“OK. That sounds easy enough,” David replied.

Omar looked at him and said, “Before we load you in the van, you must pay me.”

David handed him an envelope with $500 U.S. dollars inside. Omar looked surprised, “So you still do not trust Omar,” he replied.

“You will get the rest of your money when I am back safely at this hotel,” David said.

“OK, OK,” Omar said as he snatched the envelope. “After I leave you inside Petra, I will see you again tomorrow morning at the hotel to get the rest of my money. If I don’t get it, you will never get out of here alive,” he said firmly.

CHAPTER 8 - DAVID

David glanced at his watch as they pulled up beside a small, old minivan, wondering if he would get out of Petra alive. Omar told him to get into the back of the van. David grabbed his camera case and equipment and jumped in. It was a tight fit with all the food that was crammed into the van. The smell was strong from the spices in the food. David had to sit on his camera case and sit firmly against the side wall of the van. A wave of fear and uncertainty swept over him as the door of the van closed, blocking his sight to the outside world.

David knew that the passage they would be entering was very narrow. As they approached the entrance, the security police stopped them to inspect the van. They were probably running a mirror underneath the van to make sure there were no explosives hidden there. David prayed that no one would look in the back where he was hiding. Fortunately, the guards seemed to know Omar. David heard them laughing and then the van pulled away and slowly entered the mountain of stone called Petra. Normally, when visitors were allowed inside, they had to either walk or rent a mule or horse to ride on.

This was one of the few vehicles allowed inside the confines of this stone fortress. David decided to hide one of his remote microphones inside the van. He taped one under the back of the driver's seat hoping to be able to hear about any plots to harm him before they got an opportunity to do it. He also slipped one into Omar's backpack which was lying behind the passenger seat.

After traveling a mile inside, the van pulled over to one of the carved entrances to a stone building and came to a stop. Omar got out and walked around to the back door and opened it. "You must get out quickly and follow me," he said to David. David's legs were cramped after sitting in the small van. He stumbled and almost fell as he jumped out of the back dragging his equipment with him. Omar led him inside one of the carved rock temples and told him to walk up higher, that he should be able to get the photos he wanted from that point. He told David that he would pick him up at exactly 5:00 in the afternoon at the same entrance. David mumbled a thanks and looked around as his eyes adjusted to the subdued light inside the temple. As he surveyed his new surroundings, he saw boxes and barrels stacked against the back wall of the stone temple. He decided that he would wait until Omar was long gone before trying to see what was in the boxes and barrels.

David noticed a stairway leading up to a cave-like opening near the top of the temple and decided to explore the upper level to see if he could find a good place to set up his equipment. Near the top, he found an opening large enough for his camera to get a good wide-angle view of the surrounding area. He went back downstairs and brought his equipment to the upper level and carefully set up his camera and sound equipment. He wanted to try to capture some of the conversations that were taking place in the area in addition to the video.

It had been many years since he had visited Petra, and David searched his memory for how it was laid out. He could clearly see that things were very different now than what he remembered. The open area between the sides of the mountains was filled with equipment of some kind. It looked as though entire portable buildings had been brought inside and assembled. He assumed that it was a training area for terrorists; otherwise, why all the secrecy and why no tourists? From his training with the Israeli military, he knew it was a military installation.

In Israel, every young person must spend time in the military before going on to college or starting a career. David had been in the Army for four years and had spent most of his time in intelligence. The sights he was witnessing in Petra reminded him of his training in the military. Below him, all kinds of maneuvers were taking place with young Arab men and boys. As he listened with his intelligence gathering equipment, he heard them talking about how much they hated Americans and Israelis. Death to all infidels, they were saying.

David checked the equipment for anything the microphone he had planted in Omar's van might have picked up. He heard nothing. He planned to check every few minutes to see if he could determine what Omar might be up to. He secretly feared that he had been led into a death trap and that he would never see his country, his wife, or his children again.

David turned his attention again to what was happening below him. He used the camera equipment to try to pick up what was being said. It was obvious that there was some major training going on in Petra. It appeared to him to be a terrorist camp where young recruits were being trained to conduct terrorist raids. He tried to listen and record as much as possible of what was being said.

In school and college, he had learned to speak several languages. He could hear a man who appeared to be an instructor screaming at the young recruits. The instructor seemed very upset. As he strained to listen, he thought he heard the instructor talking about Saddam. "Saddam Hussein," he screamed, "has betrayed all of us, he did not die like a hero. He allowed the Americans to pull him out of his hole like a worm. He had a gun. Any honorable military leader would have never allowed anyone to capture him. He should not have allowed them to capture him alive. He should have killed himself. Instead, he allowed them to capture him and then hang him like a dog."

He continued ranting. "He has brought shame on Allah and all those who trusted in his leadership. We must avenge Allah by killing all infidel enemies." Then he raised his arms in the air and asked, "Who is the enemy?" And all those in the group yelled, "Death to all Zionist and Americans. Death to one and all."

David sat back, ran his fingers through his salt and pepper hair, and sighed. He knew how much they believed what they said. He lay on the floor of the small room he was in and said a prayer. He knew he was in great danger. If they found him here, he would surely be killed. They would find out that he was an Israeli reporter, and they would kill him. What have I gotten myself into? he thought.

David knew that this intense hatred would cause many deaths in Israel and perhaps America as well. So many Americans travel abroad, and they are easy targets in many parts of the world. David continued to record and to pray. He prayed that there would be a way for him to get out of there without being detected. However, he also believed that Omar was not trustworthy and that he had very little chance of surviving this trip. He searched for an internet satellite signal on his laptop, hoping to send some of the information he had collected back to Fox, but he had no luck. The high rock mountains left little chance for any signals to penetrate.

For the remainder of the day, he recorded the activities of the young militant terrorists training on the floor of Petra. As the sun set, he felt the temperature dropping so he turned his camera off and packed up his equipment, hoping that Omar would indeed come for him.

He had no food and he was very hungry. He slid back away from the entrance and walked to the back of the large cave-like interior. He saw several boxes and some metal containers stacked near the back wall. He pried the lid off one of them and noticed that it contained a powdery substance. Suddenly he realized that the mobile units below were probably portable chemical labs. He assumed that they had been dismantled at another location, brought here, and reassembled. He realized that they were making chemical weapons of mass destruction.

David scrambled back down the steps to the larger room. No one seemed to be around. He looked through a few boxes and saw nothing resembling food. Suddenly, it dawned on him that Omar was not bringing in food; he was bringing in containers of various kinds of chemicals. He realized that he was in serious trouble. Something was happening here that was much bigger than he realized. He scrambled around and found more metal containers of chemicals. The word anthrax was written in Arabic on several of the containers. David shuddered, and realized that the substance in the containers was lethal.

"Oh dear, God," said David aloud. "These chemicals are meant for my people. My wife and children could become victims of these weapons. I must find a way to report and stop this."

David looked outside and noticed that it was getting dark. He proceeded to transfer some of the still photographs he had taken during the day. Since he had a cell phone, he had email capabilities. He immediately typed a brief summary about the day's activities to send via email to Ingrid. He downloaded the photos and prayed that she would get them. He then slipped back downstairs. It was dark now. He went back upstairs. He heard Omar coming, and he heard him talking with two other people. David pretended to be asleep as he heard them coming up the steps. Omar walked over and kicked him in the side, causing severe pain. David managed to jump to his feet to try to defend himself. Omar and his companions jumped David, wrestling him to the ground and tying his hands behind his back.

"What's going on?" David asked.

Omar laughed, "You will soon see, my friend. You will soon see." They dragged David down the steps and threw him into the corner of the room. He tried to breathe but found it extremely painful. David feared Omar's kick may have cracked or broken a rib.

Omar went to the van, started the engine, and drove away. Now David feels certain his life is in danger and that he had been set up. Omar's companions went back upstairs and came back with all of his camera equipment.

"Where are you taking that?" he asked. The men didn't respond. They went outside, leaving him behind. He tries to get to his feet but is unable to stand up. He had a pocket knife attached at the top of his sock, but with his hands tied behind him, he was unable to reach it. David twisted around looking for something to use to free himself but didn't see anything. After struggling for a while and making no progress, he gave up and waited.

CHAPTER 9 - INGRID

Ingrid tried to call her mother before leaving the hotel. She is unable to reach her, so she leaves a voicemail. "Mum, it's Ingrid. I love you. I'll call you later."

Ingrid spent most of the day walking around town talking to people as though she were a tourist. She wanted to find someone locally who would trust her enough to talk to her. She wanted to see if anyone could give her information about what was going on in Petra, but so far no one wanted to talk. "We don't know why they have closed it to tourists," they all said. "If we knew, we would tell you."

It was 6:00 pm, and her feet were hurting. She headed back to the hotel thinking about taking a bath. When she got to her room, she had a strange feeling that someone had been there. She looked in the closet and bathroom, but no one was there. She looked at her luggage and noticed that one of the locks was open. She always locked it when leaving the room. She looked inside but nothing seemed to be missing. She picked up her briefcase, took out her computer, and turned it on to check emails. She is surprised to see that David has sent an email. She carefully reads his words and realizes what a dangerous situation this has become. She looked at the photos attached and felt even more concern. If anyone knows she has these, she will be in danger. She copied them onto another CD and tucked the CD into her purse. She went into the bathroom and adjusted the water to run a bath. She was expecting David to return at any moment. She stepped into the tub and hoped to stay there for a while. When she got out, it was dark outside. She dialed David's room, and a woman answered the phone. "Where is David?"

Ingrid asked in broken Arab dialect.

"No one is here by that name," she said. Ingrid got dressed and went down to the front desk. She asked for David's room number, and the clerk told her that he had checked out and left. Ingrid knew this was not true, but she didn't know what to do. She went back upstairs and tried to figure out what to do next. Feeling close to panic, she wonders what has happened to David. She hears a knock at the door. Since she cannot see outside, she asks, "Who's there?"

"Omar," came the reply. Ingrid opened the door slightly. "I am here for the rest of my money," he said.

"Where is David?" Ingrid screamed.

"He will be here tomorrow. He wanted to stay another day and get more pictures. He said you would give me the rest of my money, and he will see you tomorrow."

"I don't have your money. David had it with him when I saw him last."

"You lie," he yelled. "Give me my money, or I will come in and take it and take care of you at the same time."

She couldn't decide what to do. She didn't have Euros or dollars. All she had was shekels, so she reluctantly gave him the equivalent shekels in order to get rid of him. She thought that he had probably robbed David of the other five hundred, and then came to hustle her for the more. Omar walked out without saying a word.

She locked the door and sat back on the bed. She wished she could talk to John. She picked up her cell phone and dialed his number. Nothing happened. She picked up the desk phone and called, knowing it would not be a secure call. The phone rang several times and then she heard his voice on a recording. "Leave a message, and I'll get back to you," the voice said. "John, it's Ingrid. I'm in Jordan, and I'm having trouble making calls. I'm in serious trouble and may never get to see you again. If not, remember that I love you, John." She hung up.

Ingrid went down to the hotel restaurant and ordered dinner. When it arrived, she picked at the food for about fifteen minutes and finally gave up and left. She went back to her room and sent an email to Joel Black, her boss in Atlanta. She described the situation in Jordan and asked for his advice. Despite the time difference, she knew he would be in the office, anxious to hear from her. She also forwarded David's email and photos so Black could see what was taking place in Petra. Then she shut down her computer and fell asleep.

Ingrid's clock was set to alarm at 6:00 am, but she was already awake. She booted up her laptop to see if Joel had responded to her email. He had. He expressed his concern about Ingrid and David's safety, especially after viewing the photos. He told her that if David did not return today, she was to get out of there and go back to Amman. Once she was back in Amman, she was to call Black to discuss the next step.

She headed downstairs. She could smell the coffee before she reached the lobby. She poured a cup and picked up a bagel. Her fear and concern kept her from having much of an appetite, so the other foods didn't appeal to her.

After breakfast, she got her camera and walked around town, attempting to get more information about

Petra. She didn't have much luck. She was ready to give up when a man came up to her. "Are you the reporter from the U.S. that has been asking questions around town?" he asked.

"Yes, I am," Ingrid replied.

"Follow me to my shop," he whispered. He walked ahead of her, and Ingrid followed him into a small shop filled with all kinds of trinkets and souvenirs.

"I am very worried. You must tell people what is happening here," he said.

"What's going on?" Ingrid asked.

"The rumor is that the terrorists have brought in scud missiles and bombs and are arming them with chemicals. They plan to soon launch them at Israeli targets. If they launch scud missiles from here, we will become a target for the Israeli Air Force, and our peaceful town will be destroyed."

He continued, "King Hussein never would have allowed this to happen. But since his death, things have gone mad. There is a much-disputed rumor that Saddam smuggled chemicals of mass destruction out of Iraq just before the U.S. attacked, and they came through Syria and are being stored here in Petra. I believe that these weapons really came from Iran, not Iraq. I should not be telling you this. I could be killed if Hamas finds out that I have talked to you. They are angry since the Israeli military killed one of their leaders."

"Don't worry," Ingrid told him. "I won't let them know what we have talked about."

He looked around and suddenly told her that she must leave. He escorted her to the back of his shop and said, "Go out here."

She found herself in a small alley. She hurried back to the hotel. She felt even more frightened. The situation was much worse than she had previously thought.

She sent another quick email to Joel Black telling him what she had learned. His reply came quickly, "Get out now, Ingrid. Don't wait. Go now!" he emphasized.

She prayed that David would get back soon so they could leave together. She saw no sign of his return when she went to his room. She asked at the front desk about him, but they still weren't helpful. They were sticking with their story; "Raul said he checked out and left in a hurry."

She hurried back to the elevator and headed for her room. She checked her email again. Nothing new. She sent Joel a note and told him there was no sign of David. Next, she sent David an email and told him that she was leaving.

She paced around the room for a few minutes, thinking. She realized that she had no choice – she had to leave. She started packing, all the while trying to stay calm. She decided to leave as soon as it was dark outside. She got her map and plotted the route to Amman. She wished she had a GPS device, but David had taken it with him. According to her calculations it was 250 km from Petra to Amman through a country known as the "lonely planet." Since David had driven to Petra, she had not paid close attention to the route they had taken. She went downstairs and ordered some food to take with her on the road.

She took her things down the back stairs and found her way to the back lot where they had parked the Range Rover. She fumbled through her purse for the key and thanked God that David had left it with her. She started the engine and headed out. "This country is so desolate," she thought. When I leave the small towns, there will be nothing but barren desert with little vegetation of any kind for some distance."

She drove for three hours and then started to feel very sleepy. She pulled to the side of the road and stopped to take what she hoped would be a quick nap. She looked at the map and figured she must be close to Kerak Castle. Lonely planet indeed, this place was so lonely, it is frightening. She closed her eyes and fell asleep.

CHAPTER 10 - DAVID

David heard Omar's companions coming back. He tried to sit up, but his ribs made it too painful. The men walked in and grabbed David and pulled him upright. "OK, mister news reporter," the shorter one said. "We will have a talk now." The man smelled so bad that David had the urge to gag when he came close. They pushed/carried him deeper into the red mountain and into a tent set up near the amphitheater. They dropped him in a heap in the corner. The pain was almost unbearable.

A tall slim man with a full beard and beady brown eyes looked at David. "Why are you here?" he asked. David tried to take a breath and answer, but before he could say a word, the short one kicked him in the groin.

"You were asked a question," he yelled. Now David knew he would not be able to talk. The bearded man pulled out a long knife and said, "We have ways of making you talk."

David struggled to speak, "I am here to learn what is going on," he whispered.

"I have an idea of what to do with you," the tall man said. He called the other two outside, and David could hear them whispering to each other. Even though David couldn't hear what they were saying, he knew they were talking about what to do with him.

The tall one said to the other two, "I want you to put him in the next car loaded with explosives that is going to Israel. We don't want him here, but we cannot let him leave. We will make it look like an Israeli is responsible for our next act of retaliation."

"That is a good plan," said the short man. "You are very wise, Mohammed. Take him away then, and we will get rid of him tomorrow."

They picked David up and took him to a small room in the back of the temple. They handcuffed him to a large metal container. There were strange smells in the room. David tried to figure out what the smell was and finally decided it was an unusual chemical odor. David felt terribly sick after breathing it for a few minutes. His lungs felt like they were on fire, and he realized that he was being poisoned. After the men left, David tried to move the container, but it must have weighed several hundred pounds. He was unable to budge it. He settled back and started to drift into sleep. He caught himself and thought that he couldn't let himself fall asleep. It was too dangerous. He knew that he was in serious trouble, and he was sure the men would find a way to kill him.

As he struggled to keep himself awake, David thought about how he had always heard that people facing death see their entire life pass in front of them. His life was passing in slow motion tonight. He thought about growing up in Israel. He remembered going to school in Jerusalem and the uniforms they were required to wear. He remembered the teaching of the rabbis as they recited the Torah to the children. He remembered going to the Wailing Wall at the beginning of Sabbath and tucking a prayer into a crack in the wall as he quoted the law and the prophets.

He also remembered his childhood sweetheart, Sarah. Sarah had such beautiful long, dark hair. They were sweethearts through primary school. Then one day, Sarah did not come to school. When David asked the teacher about her, all he would say was that Sarah would not be back. David had cried at night for a long time wondering what had happened to Sarah. Then one day, he heard his father telling his mother that Sarah and her family had been killed by a terrorist bomb blast in their neighborhood.

David thought about his beautiful wife, Elizabeth. He remembered the words she had said to him many times, “Jesus is the Messiah. You should believe in him.” Elizabeth had converted to Christianity shortly after they were married. She never pushed David, but gently reminded him that the Messiah had already come and that his name was Jesus the Christ.

“Elizabeth,” he would reply, “the rabbis say that the Messiah is yet to come.”

“OK," she would say, "but I believe in Christ.”

As David lay in the dark rock tomb, he decided to pray. He prayed to the God of his fathers, and he also prayed to Jesus Christ. If my wife can believe in you, then I will also. I accept you as my Messiah. Then he slowly drifted off to sleep.

At sunrise, David was awakened and dragged out to a horse. He was tied on the horse and led out the narrow passageway. Once outside, he is put into the back of a gray van. “Where are you taking me?” David asked.

“You will see,” Mohammed said.

The van pulled out, heading off into the desert leaving behind a thick cloud of dust. Several hours later, they neared the border of Israel. The van stopped in a grove of trees, and David hears a conversation with a female. “You know what to do,” Mohammed said.

“Yes,” the female replies.

The back door of the van is opened, and David is dragged out. David is forced to walk about a mile through rough desert terrain. They finally come to what David assumes is the border. They wait until it is dark, and then force David to crawl through a ditch that is obviously manmade. The ditch takes them inside the wall. The sound of a truck coming near forces them to lay down flat and not move. The dust is so heavy that it clogs their nostrils and makes it difficult for them to breathe. The truck that passes is filled with Israeli soldiers. David and his captors can hear the soldiers talking as the truck passes. After a few minutes, the men haul David over to a car that had been covered with a large camouflage tarp. David is put into the passenger side of a dark green car, tied in such a way that he cannot move. They drive slowly out through a narrow trail. After several miles, they entered a paved road headed for Haifa.

The young woman driving the car is covered in traditional Palestine clothing. David asked her where they were going, and she didn't reply. He then asked her to let him go. He told her that he has a wife and children, but it didn't seem to faze her. She kept driving. David felt certain he was going to die, so he continued to pray. He thought about his children growing up without him. He thought of his wife and prayed that she would be OK without him.

They entered Haifa, and the woman drove to a hotel. She pulled around to the side entrance and into a parking garage. She stopped very close to the entrance of the hotel and got out of the car. David heard Israeli soldiers yelling at her to move her car. She leaned over as though getting into the car, looked sadly into David's eyes, pulled a remote-control device out of her pocket, and mashed a red button.

“Oh, dear God,” David said out loud. “They will

think an Israeli did this. They will think I am a traitor if they can identify my body. God, please take care of my family…"

She ran a few feet from the car and pressed the button on the remote. The blast shattered the hotel windows. People panicked as the first three floors of the hotel burst into flames. There were bodies everywhere. An ambulance arrived almost immediately, and the Israeli police went near the exploded car. Unfortunately, the officers concluded, there wasn't much left of the bodies. It would be impossible to identify them. A phone call was placed to the police station telling them that Hamas was responsible.

CHAPTER 11- INGRID

Ingrid was startled by a noise and then saw headlights in her rearview mirror. "Oh, dear God," she said. A vehicle was coming towards her. She had pulled off the road earlier because she felt too tired and sleepy to continue driving. She started the vehicle, put it in gear, and began driving back onto the paved road. She drove fast, but the lights were coming up behind her even faster. She couldn't think fast enough about what she should do. Stay calm, she told herself.

She slowed, hoping the vehicle behind her would pass. The car pulled up close behind her and followed for several kilometers. A little further along, a black Mercedes pulled up beside her. The back window was rolled down and a gun barrel was pointed at her. The man holding the gun waved for her to pull over. Ingrid slowed as though she was going to pull over. Then suddenly, she accelerated and turned toward the Mercedes, causing it to swerve. The driver of the car lost control and swerved back and forth across the highway. He regained control and started speeding up to catch up with Ingrid. The car pulled up beside her again. This time when the window was rolled down, the gunman fired a shot at Ingrid's tires. She lost control as her left rear tire went flat. She hit the brakes and tried to slow down. Suddenly, Ingrid's SUV turned over and she began to roll down the highway. She heard glass breaking and felt the seatbelt and shoulder harness digging into her body as the airbag exploded into her chest and everything went dark.

The driver of the Mercedes slammed on the brakes and pulled up beside the SUV which was on its top with smoke coming from the engine compartment.

“Let's go,” Omar said to Mohammed. “She will not survive this.”

Mohammed hesitated for a moment, “but what if she does survive?”

“If she shows up later, we will take care of her then. She will not cause us any problems now.”

“OK.” The driver turned the car and headed back toward Petra.

Sometime later, Ingrid saw a large knife coming inside the window of the vehicle. She screamed, and a voice spoke to her in broken English. “Hold still. I am trying to get you out of here.” The knife cut through the seatbelt and she started to fall, but two large, rough hands pulled her through the open window.

“Are you OK?” the man asked.

“I'm not sure. Everything hurts right now,” Ingrid whispered. The man pulled her over to the edge of the road and told her to lay still. Ingrid lay on the hot sand beside the pavement hurting all over. She had bits of glass in her hair and on her clothes. She tried to move her legs, but it was too painful. After a few minutes, Ingrid lost consciousness as the large man hovered over her.

The next thing Ingrid was aware of was a loud noise. She was surprised to see that she was inside a tent-like enclosure. She had no idea where she was or what time it was. Fear began to overtake her. She tried to move, but the pain was almost unbearable. She heard footsteps and saw a shadow coming near.

“Where am I?” Ingrid asked. A child moved closer to where she lay on a cot and stared at her but didn't say anything.

"Hello," Ingrid said softly. The child continued to stare for a while and then ran away. The inside of the tent smelled musty. Ingrid could also smell animals that were obviously close by outside. A few minutes later, a woman entered and walked over to her.

"You hurt," she stammered. "You hurt badly. Don't move," she said and walked to the entrance to call for someone else. "Amyl, you must come."

A man entered the tent. "What do you want?" he asked. She pointed to Ingrid. He moved over to the cot where she lay. "You awake."

"Yes," Ingrid replied. "I'm awake. But I hurt all over." "You're lucky to be here," he said. "You hurt."

"How long have I been here?" Ingrid asked.

"Three days," the man said. "You are here for three days. You call out many times."

"My side and my ribs hurt the worst. They may be broken," Ingrid said, gently touching the painful areas.

"Maybe," the man replied. "You rest. She gets you food." "Who are you and where am I?" Ingrid asked.

"We are Bedouins. We talk more when you are stronger. You stay on this side of tent. Other side for men."

Ingrid remembered learning about the Bedouins shortly after arriving in Israel. They were a nomadic people who lived in the desert and wandered from place to place for many centuries. They had their own laws and did not adhere to other laws or governments. They moved from place to place to find grazing lands for their herds. Mostly the women shepherded the herds, made crafts, cooked meals, and tended the children. The men sold the crafts to earn money to buy gasoline for the truck and the essentials to maintain their existence.

A short while later, the woman approached Ingrid with a bowl of soup. “You eat,” she said. “You eat it all.”

The child returned to watch Ingrid, and she realized the child was a girl. “Hello,” she said. This time, the young girl smiled a slight smile. “What is your name?” she asked. The girl didn't reply but smiled at her again.

She struggled to sit up so she could eat. Pain shot through her side and ribs, and she grunted. Once she was finally sitting somewhat upright, she tasted the soup. It had a strange and unusual taste. It was broth with meat and no vegetables. She guessed from the sounds of the animals outside that it was made with either sheep or goat meat. She tried not to think about it, telling herself it was probably best if she didn’t know.

The woman entered and helped Ingrid sit up a little more. She tasted the soup again. She didn’t like it very much but tried to eat it anyway. The woman handed her a piece of cheese and dried bread. Ingrid pulled off pieces of bread and ate until she was satisfied. She then gently slid back down on the cot to rest. The child was still standing beside Ingrid, watching her as she closed her eyes.

When Ingrid woke again, it appeared to be early morning. She looked around trying to remember where she was. Then it came to her. She could see several goats and a few sheep grazing outside on the rocky slope. An older girl walked in. She appeared to be in her late teens. “Hello,” she said in English.

“Hello,” Ingrid replied. “Who are you?”

"My name is Alma," she said in broken English. "I have worked for a family from London for two years. I learn bloody English very well."

"Alma, my name is Ingrid. I am happy to meet you."

"I will get married soon. I met a chap from another tribe of Bedouins, and we will be married very soon."

"Wonderful! Congratulations," Ingrid replied. "You seem like a nice young lady."

"Thank you," she said. "You want to take a bath? I will help you. We go to the stream, and you can take a bath."

"OK, that would be nice. Can you help me get on my feet?"

Alma was strong and helped Ingrid walk down the rocky path to the stream. "What is the name of this stream?" Ingrid asked her.

"This is the Jordan River. It is not very large like other rivers." It is more like a large stream, thought Ingrid. They found a shady place and waded into the water. Ingrid took off her clothes and dipped into the river. It was so hot here, and the water was warm. It soothed Ingrid's sore body. Ingrid noticed several large bruises on her side and thighs. As they walked back to the tent, Ingrid felt better.

"Have you always lived here?" Ingrid asked the girl.

"Oh, no. We wander through the desert to find places where there is food for the animals and where we can do odd jobs to make a little money for food and gasoline for the trucks. We are never in one place for more than a few months."

"Where did you meet your future husband?" Ingrid continued.

“He lives a short distance from here in another camp. His father raises and sells camels. His father and my father are friends, and they say we will marry.”

“Do you love him?” Ingrid asked.

“I don’t know. I will find out after we are married. It really does not matter; our fathers say what we must do. My father is only concerned if I am a virgin when I marry. If I do not show the signs of a virgin on my wedding night, then I have disgraced my family and my father must put me to death. I have not been with a man, but I must show the sign.”

"What are you saying?” Ingrid asked. “Your father will kill you?

“Oh, yes. It happens if a woman does not show the sign. It is the father’s obligation to stone her, for she has brought shame to the family.”

“Alma, a woman may not show the sign of a virgin for other reasons than being with a man,” Ingrid tells her. “She might have an accident or some other activity that causes her to lose the sign.”

“It does not matter,” Alma said. “If I do not show the sign, I will die. They will place a white cloth under me on my wedding night. If I show the sign of a virgin, they will take the white cloth and hang it up, and everyone will celebrate.”

They arrive back at the camp, and Ingrid is out of breath from the walk and the bath. Back inside the tent, Ingrid lay down slowly and thought about their conversation. This was a very old culture. There are no police to call for protection; the only law here was the law of the people. With this realization, Ingrid feels afraid, not knowing what may happen to her or how she will ever get out of this place and get back to Jerusalem.

After dark, Alma's family was outside around the campfire talking. Alma came into the tent where Ingrid lay. “Do you have someone your father tells you to marry?” she asked.

“Oh, no. I have a man that I love, but my father will not get to know him. My father died a few years ago. I am free to choose whom I love and want to marry,” Ingrid tells her.

“What do you mean you love him? What is this love you speak of?” asked Alma.

“Love is hard to explain. Love is a deep feeling you have inside of you that causes you to want to be with another person and take care of that person. If that person returns your love and has the same feelings for you, then you can decide to marry and spend your lives together. Love is the action of showing someone else how important they are to you.”

“It sounds strange,” Alma replied. “I am not aware of this kind of feeling for Nebula.”

“Maybe it will come in time,” said Ingrid. “You are a beautiful, sweet young lady. He is very lucky to get such a nice person to become his wife.”

Amyl showed up early the next morning. “Amyl” Ingrid asked? “Were you able to bring any of my things out of the wrecked vehicle?”

“Some of them,” he responded. “They are in the back of my truck. Someone wanted you to die; I saw someone in the black car shooting at you. I hid until they drove away. I did not take time to look for things in your car. I was afraid they would return. I went back the next day and it was gone. Someone took the car away. Come, I will show you what I have,” Amyl told her.

Ingrid struggled to her feet and walked slowly to

the truck. Amyl pulled back a cover, and Ingrid saw a piece of her luggage and a briefcase. Everything else was gone; her case that contained her cosmetics and jewelry was gone. Her computer and camera were not there. Her heart sank when she realized that her grandmother's brooch was gone. Tears pooled in her eyes and ran down her cheeks.

"I am sorry," he said.

"That's OK. Thank you for salvaging my clothes." He took her bags back to the tent, put them inside, and walked away.

Ingrid opened her luggage containing clothes and noticed that someone had gone through it. Things were rearranged. She wondered if Amyl had gone through it and kept her jewelry so he could sell it. She realized that she probably would never know. She took out fresh clothing and sat down on the side of the cot. How will I ever get back to civilization, and will I ever see John again, she wondered, feeling lonely and desolate.

CHAPTER 12 - John

It had been a very difficult day. John had just returned from an assignment in Arizona. He had caught a flight from Phoenix to Salt Lake City, and then on to Denver. He had arrived at 10:00 pm and collected his Jeep to head home. It was getting cold, and he knew that winter would arrive soon. At home, he unloaded his luggage and computer. He listened to his voice mail and trembled when he heard Ingrid's voice. The message disturbed him, but he didn't know what to do. He got a fire started in his den and turned on the TV. Local weather was reporting on a cold front moving in and snow flurries starting in the higher elevations.

Thirty minutes later, John climbed into bed with the TV on in his room. He was about to fall asleep when a reporter came on and said, "Two Fox reporters from Israel on assignment in Jordan are missing."

John sat upright and strained to hear more. Photos of Ingrid and David on location in Israel were posted on the screen. Then a picture was displayed of a wrecked vehicle that appeared to be on the back of a flat-bed truck. "This is the vehicle they rented. It was discovered by the Jordanian military in the middle of the road between Petra and Amman," the announcer was saying. "There are several bullet holes in the side of the wreckage; however, there is currently no sign of either reporter. It is thought that a terrorist group known to operate in the area may have captured them."

John lay back on the bed with tears flowing down his cheeks. My beautiful Ingrid – where are you? John thought. It is more than I can bear to think of Ingrid being harmed. He was unable to sleep, trying to develop a plan of how he could find her. "Where do I start? I feel so helpless. Oh, God, please not again. I pray, please don't let her be taken away from me." He was so afraid that this time would be the same way it had been with Katherine. He would lose her, and there was nothing he could do to stop it.

Early the next morning, John called the human resources department at Fox. "I'm sorry, sir," the lady who answered his call. "Unless you are a family member, we cannot give out any information."

"Can you tell me how to contact her family?" John pleaded. "Sir, I wish I could, but it's against our policy."

"Would you be allowed to contact them and ask them to contact me?" John asked her.

"I'll see what I can do. I'll get back to you later today."

"Thanks," John said. "I really need to talk to them."

John watched the news all day, but there were no further reports regarding Ingrid. He finally received a call late in the day from Fox.

"Mr. Martin, we have talked to Ingrid's mother in Luxembourg. She is willing to talk to you. She remembers Ingrid talking about you before she left for Israel. I will text you her address and phone number and a file photo of Ingrid before I leave today."

"Thank you so much. I really appreciate your help. If you hear anything from Ingrid, please tell her to call me as soon as possible. Thanks again," John said and hung up. Finally, he would get to talk to her family. John waited for the text and thought about what he would say to her mother when he called her.

He couldn't remember a colder time in the mountains. The howling wind and the cold air chilled him to the bone. John added more wood to the fire in his den and sat down. He was thinking about Ingrid as he smelled the aroma of burning firewood. "Oh, God," he prayed, "how I wish she could be here with me in my arms by the fire tonight."

At last John received the text with the contact information for Ingrid's mother. He dialed the number, and she answered after two rings. "Hello, Mrs. Bauer. This is John Martin calling. I am a friend of Ingrid's, and I'm calling from Denver, Colorado in the United States."

"Yes, Mr. Martin. I remember my Ingrid saying she had met a nice young man from America. We are so worried about her, Mr. Martin. Do you know what has happened to her?"

"No, Mrs. Bauer. I was hoping you had heard from her. And please, call me John."

"OK, John. I have not talked to her since she left for Jordan. She did leave a voice message at one point, but I was away when she called. I'm so sorry I missed her call. She sounded distressed. I can always tell when she is distressed. And now she is missing." Mrs. Bauer began to cry. "I didn't want her to go. I told her I was worried for her safety. She told me not to worry, but I couldn't help it."

"I know, Mrs. Bauer. I've been worried about her, too. If you hear from her, please let me know. And if I hear from her, I will let you know."

"OK, John. Please pray for her safety."

"I will Mrs. Bauer. I will keep in touch with you. Good-bye."

After the phone call, John paced back and forth

before going to his computer. He looked up Jordan, Petra, and Amman. He had no clue what he was looking for, but he wanted to know what the area was like where Ingrid had disappeared. He decided he would go there and look for her himself. He called the client for his next assignment and told them that he'd had a personal crisis arise and needed to reschedule his appointments for the following month. Next, he called the airline and booked the next available flight to Amman. He started packing but realized he didn't know how long he would be gone. So, he took several changes of clothing and headed to the airport.

John boarded the plane and collapsed into the seat. He felt like he was in a daze. He tried to read *USA Today*, but got bored with it after a few minutes. He gave up and closed his eyes and attempted to sleep but was unable to do so. Hours later, he was still awake and watching the airplane fly across the ocean on the map on the screen.

The seat beside John was open, so he raised the armrest and lay down. He was soon dreaming of finding Ingrid in the desert land of Jordan. He saw her and ran to her. She had tears running down her cheeks as she jumped into his arms. John woke up and realized that it was only a dream.

Twelve hours later, John was getting off the plane in Jordan. He suddenly realized that he had no clue where to go or how to begin his search. He rented a car and asked for a map and directions to a nice hotel. He weaved his way through very confusing streets and found the hotel on the side of a hill overlooking downtown.

He checked in, got to his room, and asked himself what to do next. After unpacking, I went back to the lobby and asked for directions to a convenience store. He walked around the corner and up the hill to find a small shopping center. He went inside and walked around. Everything seemed so strange. He didn't have a clue what people were saying. His rental didn't have a GPS, so he tried to find a map of the country that was printed in English. After looking in several stores, he found a small bookstore. He went inside and asked the clerk if she spoke English. He was relieved when she smiled and said, "a little."

Together, they found a map that John could read, and she showed him where Petra was located. She then highlighted the route so John could more easily find it. John told her how much he appreciated her help. "You're welcome," she said. John walked back to the hotel and went to his room to study the map until he was confident that he knew where to go the next morning.

CHAPTER 13 – INGRID & ALMA

“Alma, where are we?” Ingrid asked.

“I'm not sure exactly,” she responded. "We are somewhere in Syria.”

“Syria!” Ingrid exclaimed. “Syria? How did we get into Syria?”

“My father crossed the border with you when he brought you here. The border guards know him, so they do not search the truck and find you.”

“I can’t believe this,” Ingrid said.

“Is that bad?” Alma innocently asked. “Syria is full of terrorists,” Ingrid replied.

“We have terrorists everywhere in this part of the world,” Alma stated. “They will not bother us, I think. We have nothing they want.”

“But Alma, how will I get out of here and back to Israel?” “You are Israeli?” she asked with surprise.

“No,” said Ingrid, “but that is where I am assigned to work.” “Ingrid, where is your home?” she asked.

“I am from Europe; from a small country called Luxembourg.”

“I don’t know about that place,” she said. “Alma, when will your father return?” “Soon,” she said. “He comes before night.”

“When he comes, will you ask him if we can speak?”

“Yes, I will tell him when he comes.”

It was almost dark when Amyl came into the tent. “You want to see me?” he asked.

"Yes. I was wondering when I can return to my home?” “You get well. We will talk then.”

"I think I am well enough to leave now," Ingrid insisted.

"You are not well, yet," he said. "You must stay for the wedding in four days." With this, he turned and walked out.

Ingrid was worried that he might never let her leave alive. How would she ever get out of Syria? She had no idea where she was in Syria, or how far it was to the border, or even which direction to go to reach the border. Besides, all her money, passport and credit cards had been left in the vehicle that was now gone. How could she rent another car or buy a plane ticket? She was sure Fox would take care of everything if she could manage to contact them.

Over the next few days, Ingrid felt stronger and the pain from the accident was easing. Preparations for Alma's wedding were under way. The wedding festivities would last for a total of three days. Several tents were set up around Amyl's tent, and colorful pieces of cloth and flags were hung from the tents as a sign of the coming celebration.

Ingrid was preoccupied with helping Alma as she prepared for the ceremony. She had chosen a more colorful dress than her normal attire. She wore a gold belt around her waist for decoration. The weddings were obviously a big deal for the families of both tribes. As the sun was setting on the evening prior to the ceremony, goats and sheep were slaughtered, and Alma's mother and many cousins began preparing food.

Alma came to Ingrid's tent and sat down. "I am so afraid," she said.

"What are you afraid of?" Ingrid asked her.

"I want to make a good wife for Nebula, my new husband." "Oh, Alma. I'm sure you will be a good wife. You know how to cook, and you know how to care for the family because you have cared so well for your younger brothers and sisters."

"Yes, I know. But what if I don't please him? What if I don't show the sign of a virgin?"

"Why would you think you might not show the sign of a virgin? Have you been with someone else?"

"No, no!" she said. "I have never been with a man."

"Then you have nothing to worry about," Ingrid assured. "I hope you are right," she responded.

"Don't worry. Any man would be pleased to have you for his wife. You are so beautiful and kind." Alma blushed, pulled the covering over her face, and slipped out of the tent.

Ingrid didn't tell her that she too was concerned for her. Ingrid had heard for many years about the female genital mutilation that occurred when the girls are about eight years old. She knew that the rest of the world considered this a barbaric practice. Yet to the Bedouin, if it was not done, the girl was considered unclean and immodest.

The next day, everyone was up very early making final preparations. The sheik who was head of the tribe would bless their marriage. The day passed in a whirlwind. The festivities lasted far into the night while the men danced around the fire.

The women sat together and talked. Coffee and tea were served around the fire all night long. At one point, Ingrid noticed that one of the young men from Nebula's tribe was staring at her. Later, Ingrid saw him talking with Amyl. She had no idea what they were saying, but the looks she was getting made her nervous.

After the wedding ceremony had ended and the

bride and groom had gone to their tent, Amyl came to the door of Ingrid's tent and asked her to walk outside. As Ingrid walked outside, she was blinded by the setting sun. Amyl said, "The young man from Nebula's tribe wants you for his wife. He will pay a handsome price to me if you marry him."

Ingrid was stunned and afraid to say anything. Finally, she pulled her thoughts together enough to say, "There is already someone I am pledged to – an American." She had a quiver in her voice but continued, "When I leave here, we plan to marry."

"But if you don't leave here, you would need a husband here." Amyl said. "We have many Bedouin men who marry women from Europe. You could marry Jared and live here forever. You would like it."

"Please. Let me have some time to think," she said.

"You have three days. He will be back in three days with a handsome dowry for me, and you will marry him then." With this, he turned and walked away.

Ingrid went back inside the tent and started sobbing. What could she do? She loved John. She wanted to get out of this place but didn't know how to get away. She made up her mind that she would find a way.

Ingrid was awakened the next morning by a noise outside. People were yelling and screaming. She went to the door of the tent and looked out. Alma was there, lying on the ground. Her new husband was holding a piece of white cloth and waving it in front of Amyl saying, "She is not a virgin. See the cloth is not stained. I have been tricked."

Amyl took the cloth and examined it. Next, he

looked at Alma and said, “You have brought shame to our family.” He grabbed her by the arm, pulled her up, and started walking away with her. Ingrid ran out of the tent and raced after them. She screamed at Amyl, “Leave her alone. There are many reasons why she might not show the sign. It could even be from riding a camel or horse, or any number of things. It does not mean she has been with a man.”

“You go back,” Amyl said to Ingrid. “You go back.”

“What are you going to do to her,” Ingrid screamed at him. “She has brought shame and disgrace to our family. She must die. She knows this,” he said. “It is the only honorable thing for me to do.”

“No,” Ingrid screamed. “Leave her alone! She is a good woman. She has not disgraced her family.”

“You do not understand our ways.” He pulled a pistol from his garment, pointed it at Ingrid, and said, “You go back now.”

Ingrid grabbed at his arm, and he knocked her down with his pistol. Two young men from the camp ran up and held Ingrid. She burst into tears, “No! no! no!” she screamed. “Don't kill her.”

Amyl continued walking, pulling Alma with him.

Alma didn't say a word. She had resigned herself to her fate. They went behind a stand of Joshua trees, and Ingrid heard a shot. Everyone was silent. It was a long moment of silence, and Ingrid couldn't even hear herself breathing. She knew that in the old days, Amyl would have had to stone Alma to death. At least a bullet was faster and more merciful, thought Ingrid. Finally, Amyl returned carrying Alma in his arms. She is silent and motionless; she is dead. Amyl placed her body on a table outside the tent. “It is done,” he said as he turned and walked away. Alma's mother, with tears running down her cheeks, dropped to her knees beside Alma's lifeless body and heaved with silent sobs.

A short time later, other women came and picked up the body of the young bride and carried her away to prepare her for burial. The burial ceremony was simple. A stone was placed at the head and foot of the grave, and a prayer was given in their Muslim tradition. Then everyone walked away.

Ingrid walked over to the grave and stood motionless, tears running down her cheeks. What kind of people were they, she asked herself? What kind of father would kill his own daughter? At that moment, Ingrid realized that tradition was far more important than human life to these people. She also realized that unless she could find a way to escape, her life would feel worthless if she were forced to marry into such a rigid culture.

She wondered if the police would arrest Amyl. Then she realized that there was no law except their own. They were a law unto themselves. No legal system from outside would interfere with their ancient tribal system. They were only accountable to their God.

Ingrid went back into the tent to think about how she could escape. She must first figure out where she was and in which direction she would have to go to get away. If she got away and was captured by other Syrian groups, her fate would be as bad or worse than if she stayed. She knelt beside the cot and started to pray.

CHAPTER 14 - JOHN

The clock was set to alarm at 6:00 am. John reached over to turn it off as it buzzed and tried to remember where he was. So often in his business, he found himself in a different place, waking up and trying to remember where he was. Many times, he would be sitting in a restaurant and would have to think about which city he was in at that point. This was the life of a lonely road warrior.

He focused his thoughts on why he was here. He was not here on a consulting assignment; he was here to find Ingrid, the love of his life. He packed and went downstairs for breakfast. Like many hotels in the United States, there was a breakfast buffet. However, the selections were very different. They had a greater variety of breads and other items like smoked fish, luncheon meats, and a variety of cheeses. He selected, ate rapidly, and headed for the rental car.

He pulled out the maps, laid them on the front seat, and headed for Petra. He couldn't believe how desolate the country was after leaving Amman. He drove through small villages that were in shambles from the endless wars and fighting in the region. He saw lots of young men sitting by the roadside looking aimless. It was obvious that they had very little to do and little purpose in life. Because of this, John knew that he was on a dangerous mission. The young men might become violent if they saw an opportunity to get money. John saw how they stared at him as he drove past, so he stayed focused on the road ahead and did not stop. He began to wish that he had brought more food and supplies with him. A person sure didn't drive 100 kilometers here and find a McDonald's on every corner. He knew he would be lucky to find a safe place to buy any food at all.

Several hours later John arrived at Petra. He searched for a hotel that looked safe. He finally selected one, went inside, and checked in. He had a photo of Ingrid that her sister Rebecca had emailed to him the week before. He showed it to the desk clerk and asked if she had seen her. “No. I have not seen this lady,” she said. “She is very pretty though.”

John asked, “What other hotels are here?” She wrote the names on a piece of paper and handed it to John. He scanned it and saw only two names. The names meant nothing to him. He took his luggage to the room and then headed back downstairs.

"Could you give me directions to the other two hotels on this list?" he asked. It was not a large town, so he walked down the street to one of the hotels on the list. He went inside and showed the photo to the clerk. He noticed the man's name tag said "Raul."

“Have you seen this woman?” John asked.

“Yes. She was here several days ago. She has been gone for at least a week,” the clerk told him in broken English. Most of the people here learned English because of the many tourists who came to visit the ancient city.

“What about the man that was with her?” John asked.

“He left before the woman,” he said. “I don’t know where he went, but someone came in and picked up his things a few days before the lady left.”

“Do you know who picked up his things?” John asked.

“Omar was his name," Raul replied.

“Could you tell me where I might find him?” John asked. "I do not know where he is.”

“Could you tell me what he looks like?” John asked.

"Like most people here. He is short, dark skinned and has black hair."

John asked about the vehicle David and Ingrid had been driving but Raul said he knew nothing about it. John thought about the fact that he should have asked at the airport. When he got back to the hotel, he planned to call the rental car agencies to see if he could find out what kind of car they had rented. He recalled the picture on the news report with the wrecked SUV, but it wasn't possible to identify the vehicle from that shot.

John decided to walk around the shops, showing Ingrid's picture and asking if anyone had seen her. He also asked people if they knew or could tell him where to find Omar. After visiting a few shops, it was obvious that he would find out very little. Apparently, Omar was a very common name. John walked into one shop and showed the picture. He noticed the odd look on the shopkeeper's face and knew that he had seen her. "No," the man said. "I do not see her." John was certain that he was lying.

"Are you sure?" John asked as the man turned to walk away. John followed him to the back of the shop.

"I cannot talk to you now," the man said softly. "You come back tonight, and we talk."

"OK. I'll be back," John replied and left the shop.

He went back to the hotel to get the rental car to drive to the entrance to Petra. He was stopped at the entrance by guards armed with machine guns. "You cannot enter," they said.

"I am looking for Omar," said John.

The guard frowned and said, "I don't know this Omar you speak of or who he is." It was obvious that he was not telling the truth. John knew enough not to argue with him, so he turned the car around and drove away.

He went back to the hotel to unpack. He immediately noticed that his luggage had been opened. When he looked through the contents but didn't notice anything missing. He knew that he couldn't make any mistakes here or he would never get out alive.

He took a shower and then called the rental agencies at the airport. Finally, he located one that had a record of a dark green Land Rover being rented to two people. "David and Ingrid are correct," the clerk said, although she refused to give their full names. "The vehicle has been totally destroyed," she said.

John hung up and headed downstairs. He asked about restaurants and went around the corner to one that was recommended. By the time he finished his meal, it was nearly dark, so he headed back toward the shop. When he got to the shop, he discovered that it was closed but the door was not locked. John opened the door and walked inside. The man that he had talked to earlier appeared from a small side room.

"I must not be seen talking to you," the man said.

The man led him to the side room and proceeded to tell John that Ingrid had been there a few days earlier. He can't remember exactly how many – maybe a week or two.

"I told her that I suspected that chemical weapons were being stored in Petra, and that I was afraid that they would be used against Israel. If that happened, Israel would attack and destroy our peaceful town."

"Did you see her cameraman, David Friedman?" John asked.

"No, but I believe that somehow he got into

Petra. I heard on the street that he did not return." he continued. "I do not know where the lady went or where she is now. That is all I know. Please, you must leave now," he said as he started leading John to the back door. John heard him lock it after it closed.

John wondered what David and Ingrid had found. If there were chemical weapons, where did they come from? Not Iraq, he hoped. Why would chemical weapons be here unless there was terrorist activity? "Oh, dear God. I pray that terrorists didn't capture Ingrid and David," he said out loud.

John went back to the hotel room and fell across the bed. He was exhausted. A few hours later, he woke up when he heard the door rattling. Someone was trying to get in. He grabbed an ashtray, the only weapon available, and stood behind the door. John realized he was trembling with fear as he heard footsteps walking away. Whoever it was had left when they found the door locked. John got back into bed after pushing the dresser in front of the door. He didn't sleep very much afterward. Every little sound woke him up.

The alarm went off and John grabbed it and jumped up. He headed into the bathroom to shower and shave. He then packed his things and went to the front desk to check out. He had decided he would not spend another night in this place.

He decided to go back to the shop and ask the shopkeeper a few more questions. When he got there, the store wasn't open, so he walked around to the back door. It was open slightly, so he pushed it open further and went inside. As he stepped inside, his foot slipped on something, and he looked down and saw something wet. As his eyes adjusted to the dimness of the room, he walked over to the counter and looked behind it. There lay the shopkeeper's body on the floor. The man's throat had been cut, and it appeared that he had been dead for some time. John ran out of the shop, jumped into the car, and took off. He could hardly breathe as he thought about what he had just seen and realized how much his own life was in danger.

By noon, John was driving back toward Amman. He decided to drive around a little in each small village along the way to see if there were any signs of the Land Rover. The first two were so small that it took him less than fifteen minutes each. The third one was a little larger. As he drove around slowly, he suddenly realized that he was being followed. A black Mercedes was behind him. He attempted to lose it as he drove from street to street but couldn't shake it. He knew nothing about how to drive in a high-speed chase. It would have been useless anyway with the short, narrow streets. So, he decided to try a different tactic. He stopped in the middle of the town on the main street, got out, and walked back to the black Mercedes. The driver's window rolled down, and a man looked at him. "What are you doing here?" the man asked.

"Looking for a friend," John replied.

"Who is your friend?" he asked

John pulled the picture out of his pocket and showed it to the man. "Have you seen this woman?" he asked.

"Yes," he said. John noticed the man's expression change to one of sadness. "I saw her some time ago, but I have been told that she is dead. I believe that she had an accident, and the police said she died from the injuries she received in the wreck."

John felt like he had been punched. "Are you sure?" he asked.

"I'm sorry to have to tell you this," the man said.

Tears filled John's eyes. He could barely see to get back to the car as he walked away. As he gets in the car, tears roll down his cheeks, but he reminds himself that can't lose control. As he drives away, the Mercedes follows him to the edge of town and turns around. He heads back to Amman, giving up his search for the Land Rover.

CHAPTER 15 - Ingrid

Ingrid awoke early the next morning, hearing voices coming from the men's side of the tent. She strained to hear what they were saying. "She will marry Jared," she heard Amyl say. "He will pay a handsome price to be able to marry a woman from Europe."

Ingrid slipped back to her cot and noticed that the other women seemed to still be sleeping. She knew that she must leave soon but didn't know which way to go. She slipped outside and walked down to the river. The river flows toward Israel, she said to herself. All she had to do was follow the river in the direction it was flowing. She had no passport, no identification, and no way to prove her identity. She would have to figure out how to get past the border guards. She decided that she would worry about that later.

She walked back to the tent after washing her face. She would have to find some food and hide it. She dug through her only remaining bag and selected a pair of sneakers and a couple of outfits that are lightweight and easy to pack. She found a small cosmetic bag, emptied it, and stuffed the clothes inside. She then went back to the cot and pretended to be asleep until she heard the other women getting up.

As the women headed outside, Ingrid pretended to be having a lot of pain and said that she didn't feel well. They left her in the tent alone. Ingrid had noticed that Alma's mother's eyes were puffy and swollen from crying most of the night. Ingrid was sure that she would not want Amyl to see her tears.

After they left, Ingrid gathered the cosmetic bag she had packed and a bottle that she could use to get water from the river. The river was shallow, and she had no idea if the water was safe to drink. But she had no choice; it would be her only way to have drinking water. It was so hot in the middle of the day that she wouldn't survive long without water.

After a few minutes, Ingrid went outside. The women had prepared some food and the men were gathering around to eat. Ingrid carefully filled her plate with bread and cheese and a few pastries left over from the wedding. She walked back inside and stuffed it in the cosmetic bag. A few minutes later, after the men had left, Ingrid went back outside and got another plate of food. Alma's mother looked at her with a questioning look, but she said nothing. As Ingrid went back inside the tent, Alma's mother followed her. "You must leave here," she told Ingrid. "You were kind to Alma, and she liked you very much. I will help you. Tonight, you must leave. I will show you which way to go to get back to Israel. You can follow the Jordan River," she whispered.

Ingrid didn't tell her that she had already figured that out. Instead, Ingrid took her hand and squeezed it. "Thank you," she said. Alma's mother turned and left, and Ingrid continued packing the food. Later, she brought Ingrid more food and a larger bag for carrying her few belongings. Ingrid told her that she could have the remaining things Ingrid was leaving behind. She was so heartbroken over Alma that things held little meaning to her now. Ingrid also now realized that material possessions held little meaning for her either. It was true that money cannot buy the most important things in life – like freedom.

Alma's mother said, "When it gets dark, I will show you." Ingrid waited in the tent until sunset when Alma's mother came into the tent, picked up Ingrid's bag, and carried it outside as though it was her own. Ingrid followed her. They walked down to the river. There were two small burros tied near the water's edge. “You ride this animal and follow the river,” she said pointing south. She reached inside her pocket and pulled out something that looked familiar. Somehow, she had gotten Ingrid's wallet and passport. “Amyl had these things,” she said.

Ingrid hugged her and told her, “I am so sorry about Alma. I know that she was a good woman.”

Tears started to flow as she continued, “Follow the river, and go quickly.”

Ingrid climbed on the back of the burro and slowly rode away. She looked back to wave at the older woman, but she was busy brushing away the tracks made by the burro that Ingrid was riding. Ingrid realized that she was going to ride the other burro upriver so that when Amyl realized that Ingrid had gone and started searching for her, he would go in the opposite direction.

The burro walked with a steady walk for several hours following the river. Ingrid had not ridden a horse in years and soon realized that riding the burro would not help her soreness from the accident. However, she knew that she must endure the pain if she was going to survive. After another hour of riding, Ingrid was unable to ignore the discomfort any longer. She got off the burro and walked, leading the animal by his rope tether. Walking was also painful, but she managed to walk for an hour and then decided to rest. She found a place where she could tie the burro to some sagebrush. Ingrid spread the blanket from the burro’s back on the ground and lay down on it.

A short time later, Ingrid heard a noise that sounded like a large truck. She didn't want to be discovered so she didn’t move. She looked in the direction of the sound and saw a large, green military-type truck crossing the river. She couldn't take the chance of thinking they would help her, so she didn’t move until after the truck had disappeared in the distance.

After a short rest, Ingrid got up and tried riding the burro again. She quickly realized that walking was less painful, so she ate a little bread and cheese from the bag as she led the burro.

The sun was getting hotter, and Ingrid's pace started to slow. She knew, however, that she couldn't stop because Amyl would not be fooled for long. She continued walking throughout the hot afternoon. Occasionally, she stopped for a brief rest and would drink some water and wash her face and arms to try to cool down.

She heard a noise and froze in her tracks. It sounded like a horse or camel moving toward her. Ingrid began to panic as she looked around and saw no place to hide. She did see a hillside not too far away, so she climbed onto the burro's back, rode across the river, and headed for the hillside. The terrain she was crossing was mostly rock, so she prayed that it would be difficult for anyone to track her. She noticed what appeared to be a cave as she approached the hillside. She rode toward the cave, dismounted at the entrance, and led the burro inside.

The entrance was small, but inside there were several tunnels going in different directions. She chose one and went as far back as she could go. The sound of riders coming across the river echoed off the cave walls. Ingrid crawled back to the entrance and looked outside. The riders were going quickly past the cave. Ingrid didn’t think they had noticed her. She saw as the group passed that it was Amyl and his sons. After they passed by, Ingrid grabbed the burro's reins and headed outside. When she reached the river, she guided the burro into the water and continued for some distance to hide their tracks.

After a couple of miles, they left the river and found a road. As she rode, she continued to look for a hillside hoping to find another cave. She finally located a small cave and quickly went inside. She prayed once more that her trail was hidden well enough so that Amyl could not find her. Thank goodness there were so many caves in this part of the world. Some of them, like the one that had contained the Dead Sea Scrolls, had not been visited for hundreds of years.

Ingrid stayed inside the cave for an extra day. Near the end of the second day, she again heard horses. She slowly moved to the mouth of the cave and carefully looked outside. She saw Amyl go by heading back towards their camp. They were moving quickly and were soon out of sight. Ingrid hoped and prayed that she would never see Amyl again.

Early the next morning, Ingrid mounted the burro and continued her journey, following the river downstream. She traveled for several hours and saw what looked like a village ahead. She was unsure where she was, so she moved close to the village and stopped. She was afraid to enter the village during the daytime and decided to hide out where she had stopped until dark.

As soon as it was dark, she mounted the burro, pulled a scarf over her face, and started riding. She rode through what appeared to be a back street. People were walking around, but most of them paid her no attention. She saw a sidewalk vendor selling figs and other fruits. She had little money and what she did have was either Euros or Israeli currency, neither of which would be accepted here.

She decided to try trading her wristwatch for some figs and any other food that she could find. She walked over and looked at the fruit and noticed that they also had freshly baked bread. She asked the man if he would trade some food for her watch. She held it out and he took it and looked it over. At last, he nodded his head and indicated that she could pick out some food. Ingrid picked up a bag and filled it with figs, other fruit, and two loaves of bread. She picked up a bottle of water and was reaching for a candy bar when the man grabbed her arm and shook his head. She understood that he felt she had taken enough in exchange for the watch.

She packed the food in the bag tied to the burro, climbed on, and rode away. Some young men followed her to the edge of the village, but no one said anything. She was soon in the wilderness again, walking beside the burro and the river.

As the sun began to set, Ingrid found a place to tie the burro. She ate some of the fruit and drank water. She leaned back against a rock and fell asleep. When the warmth of the sun hit her face the next morning, she woke up, gathered her things, and continued her journey.

After a while, Ingrid saw ahead of her a line of vehicles near a bridge and several soldiers. She apparently had reached the border. She walked a little closer and watched as the soldiers ran mirrors under the cars and buses in line checking for bombs. Ingrid noticed that the soldiers had one young man leaning over his car, and they were searching him.

It was obvious that they were doing a thorough search of people and vehicles waiting to cross. Ingrid finally walked up to the guards and showed them her passport. "Your passport is not stamped to allow you into Syria. How did you get into our country?"

"I was kidnapped," she replied, "by a Bedouin tribe and carried across the border in the back of their truck."

"How do we know this is true?" one of the young guards asked.

"I am a news reporter for Fox News." She showed him her She immediately realized that she had made a big mistake. The guard took her inside the guard hut and asked to see her camera and story. Ingrid told him that she had no camera, and he insisted on having her searched. When he was satisfied that she didn't have a camera, computer, or any other written documents, he picked up a phone and placed a call. Ingrid heard him explain the situation to the person on the other end. The guard hung up and escorted Ingrid outside to a police car and placed her inside. A policeman climbed in the front seat and drove off.

A few minutes later they pulled up in front of a military-style building, and the driver helped Ingrid out of the car and escorted her inside. An older soldier yelled at her, saying she was a spy and started asking her a lot of questions. She repeatedly told him that she was no spy, but he didn't seem to believe her. "What were you looking for?" he asked.

"Nothing," Ingrid insisted. "I was captured and carried here after I had an accident."

"You will tell us what we want to know," he insisted. "We will put you in prison." He then ordered some men to take her away.

She was taken to a facility in the desert with high stone walls with razor wire around the top. A large, hand-painted sign on the fence at the entrance to the prison read "." Ingrid was taken inside, stripped of her clothing, and given a pair of red pants and a loose-fitting shirt. All her belongings were taken, and she was escorted down a long narrow hall with a barred door at the end. The soldier unlocked the door and shoved her into a room with four other women. Ingrid was shaking all over. She was afraid she would never get out of the place. The guard yelled at her as he turned to leave, “We don’t like spies here.”

The other cell occupants looked at her suspiciously. Finally, one of them asks, “Who do you spy for?”

“I am not a spy. I am a reporter, and I was kidnapped and brought here,” Ingrid said, fighting the urge to be sick.

“All reporters are spies,” a young, dark-haired woman said and turned away from her. Ingrid looked around and noticed a small cot that seemed to be unclaimed and sat down. She started to cry. She couldn’t believe this was happening and was afraid she might not ever get out of there.

CHAPTER 16 - JOHN

John arrived back in Amman and checked into the same hotel he had stayed in before. He felt hopeless over his failure to find Ingrid. He knew that he may never find where Ingrid was buried. He had lost the love of his life.

He fell across the hotel bed and spent the night there. The next day, he woke up and realized that he should leave. After getting dressed, he packed and headed for the airport. He went through security and headed for the boarding gate. He went through security again at the gate and finally got on the plane headed home.

John gazed out the window as the plane banked to the right and headed toward Europe. He had purchased a ticket to Belgium so that he could go to Luxembourg and tell Ingrid's mother what he had learned.

As the plane climbed, John could see across the border into Syria. He noticed what appeared to be a prison off in the distance. What a terrible place for anyone to be, he thought as the plane moved into the clouds. His heart was hurting as he flew away from the place where the woman he loved would remain forever.

After a few hours, the plane landed in Brussels. John rented a car and drove across the border into Luxembourg. There were no border guards in most of Europe today. The border stations were empty, and the borders were open to free travel inside countries belonging to the European Union. How he wished the rest of the world were like this. Such beautiful, lush countryside seemed gloomy to him today. The trip he was making was filled with dread.

He arrived in Ettelbruck and drove around until he found the address sent to him by the Fox HR department. He pulled up in front of the row of houses where Ingrid had lived as a child. He went to the door and knocked. An elderly woman, an older version of Ingrid, came to the door. Behind her was someone that John guessed was Ingrid's sister. "Hello. I'm John," he said as they opened the door. "I'm so sorry to come here unannounced, but I felt I should talk to you in person. I don't have good news."

Tears began to slide down their cheeks as John told them what he learned, and that Ingrid had died in the auto accident. He recounted his experience in Jordan and the incident with the men in the black Mercedes.

"It is a rough country," he said. "I wish that she had never gone there. That country is too dangerous and violent for anyone who isn't familiar with it. I tried to find her and bring her home," John continued. He was trying to be strong in front of them but finally gave in to tears that now flowed down his cheeks.

Ingrid's mother looked at John and whispered, "Tears are a language that God understands."

Rebecca looked at John and said, "We know that you did your best to find her. We are grateful."

"We know you tried. Ingrid would be grateful to you as well," her mother said. "We know that you loved her. We are so grateful that you at least tried to find her. It is better to know the truth than to never know what really happened."

They spent several hours talking about Ingrid and how much they all loved her. Ingrid's mother showed John her childhood bedroom that was filled with memorabilia. He saw pictures of her when she was in elementary and secondary school. He saw a picture of her when she played soccer. Her team had won the championship her senior year, her mother told him.

Finally, John walked to the door and told Ingrid's family good-bye. He felt a part of himself wither as he drove out of town past the statue of General George Patton and the American tank that sat at the city limits.

John went straight to the airport in Brussels to catch a flight home. He was so tired that he didn't eat. The flight was rough and hit turbulence several times as they crossed the Atlantic. John reclined his seat and fell asleep. When he awoke, he watched the screen showing the airplane slowly making its way over Greenland, then down the U.S. coast until it landed in Atlanta. He made a connecting flight to Denver.

The next day when he was back in Denver, he went to the kennel to pick up his animal friends. They were always happy to see him. The dogs jumped and licked his hand as he loaded them into the Jeep. Bear moans and grunts as John rubs his head and ears. They traveled up the side of the mountain. John missed these snow-covered mountains when he was away.

This time, things seem different – more lonely, remote, and distant. These mountains were his refuge, but today they seemed more like a lonely tomb. He unlocked the door and went inside to build a fire and sit by the fireplace. John turned on the radio, leaned back, and closed his eyes for a moment. When he opened them, he gazed into the fire as the flames consumed the logs, and he thought about Ingrid. A group named Little Texas comes on the radio. They were singing about "what might have been." John thought about Katherine and Ingrid, and tears flooded his eyes. The pain of love lost again was so deep that he didn't think he would ever recover from it. He walked to the door, opened it, and gazed out over the mountains. "What might have been" kept running through his mind. "What might have been," he whispered to himself. He closed the door, wondering what the future could possibly bring that might help him feel joy again? The mountains had long been his home, and he was home alone again.

CHAPTER 17 - INGRID

The guard unlocked the door to Ingrid's cell and pulled her out by grabbing her arm and yelling, "Let's go. You are in trouble lady." He took her into the interrogation room and pushed her into a chair. Her heart dropped when she spotted her old laptop computer on the table. She had not seen it since it was stolen from the wrecked Land Rover.

Jamul, the head guard, looked at her with a sneer on his face. "Do you recognize this computer?" he yelled.

"I'm not sure," she responded. "May I open it and look at it?"

"You can open it, but I can tell by the look on your face that you recognize it."

She opened it slowly and turned it on. When the screen lit up, she realized that they had somehow found her computer. Her heart sank again because she was sure that they had found the photos from David Friedman showing the chemical weapons stored in Petra.

"It is mine," she responded. "Where did you find it?"

"One of our guards bought it from a Bedouin named Amyl. He found out you were a prisoner here and brought it in and showed it to the chief of the guards, who sent it to me right away. When we saw what was inside, it confirmed our belief that you are a spy. How did you take these pictures in Petra?" he demanded. With a fierce scowl, he slammed his fist on the table and yelled, "How did you know that Petra was a terrorist training camp?"

"I didn't take them. My cameraman took them

and sent them to me," Ingrid told him.

"Lies, no more lies," he yells.

"I'm not lying," Ingrid said through sobs. "Someone named Omar escorted him into Petra. Omar was supposed to bring him out, but David never returned. That's all I know."

"A likely story," Jamul said. "Who is this man named John? He was seen around Petra asking about you and showing a picture of you to shopkeepers."

"John is a man that I plan to marry," she responded.

"We do not believe you," he said. "He was your contact. We think he was here to carry information back to the Americans and Israelis."

"No! No!" she said, shaking her head. "John has nothing to do with my work."

"If you are not willing to tell us the truth, you can stay here until you die," Jamul continued. "We don't mind having you in our little hotel here in Paradise."

"Hotel!" she exclaimed. "This is a hellhole. This place isn't even good enough to call a prison. You cannot keep me here without a trial."

Jamul said with a sneer, "You will see. We will keep you here if we want to. No one knows where you are. Most people think you are dead."

Ingrid knew that what he said was right, so she looked at him and yelled, with tears running down her face, "I am telling you the truth. That is all I know."

"Guard," Jamul yelled, "take her back to the cell. We will have to show her how we treat people who do not tell us the truth."

Back in the small cell where Ingrid had been jailed for several months, she thought about what Jamul said. No one knew where she was. She felt certain that John had given up looking for her by now. Everyone probably did think that she was dead. She felt as though she might as well be dead as to be in this horrible place.

Ingrid's cellmate, Lydia, was from Israel. Lydia had been imprisoned there for five years. She told Ingrid that she had no hope of being released. She had been accused of being a terrorist, but Lydia said her only crime was accidentally crossing the Syrian border with her husband. They had been looking for a community near the border of Israel where some of their relatives lived and wandered across the border without realizing it. When the Syrian army found them, her husband had been shot immediately. Lydia had been raped, beaten, and brought here. She had been told her three children – ages 6, 8, and 11 – had been released and sent back to Israel. She cried every day as she thought about her children without either of their parents to take care of them. Ingrid felt sorry for her, as well as herself. She worried about John and what his life might be like. And she worried about her mother and Rebecca. How will they handle life without knowing what has happened to me?

This area of the world was so hot and dry, and Ingrid hated the food they were given, if you could call it food. She questioned her strength and ability to survive. At times, she felt like she was losing her mind. The only person she talked to daily was Lydia, and she was close to losing her own mind with worry about her children. There was no radio, no TV, no newspapers. She knew nothing about what was going on in the world. The only things she knew were the little bits they were told by the guards, and she was pretty sure they couldn't be trusted.

The prison smelled rancid; she found it hard to describe. There were hundreds of prisoners in the hot, desert prison. Prisoners could take a shower once a week and they took them in shifts. Every building was full of hot, smelly bodies. There was no deodorant or shampoo. They only had blocks of cheap soap. Medical care was almost non-existent. Ingrid prayed that she would not get sick.

The prisoners who had been here for years prayed that they would get sick and die. Most of them believed that death was the only way out. The week before, a woman in the cell next to Ingrid had died. The guards had taken her out in a black bag and buried her behind the prison. Ingrid could see through the window as a shallow grave was dug and the body dumped inside.

Ingrid looked forward to nighttime when the temperature was a little cooler. The prisoners slept on cots filled with straw. The beds were not comfortable, but she was so tired that she didn't care. She lay down at night, said a prayer that someone would find her and get her out, and then fell into an exhausted sleep. Sometimes, she dreamed of John and Luxembourg. When she woke up and realized it was only a dream, she would cry. The dreams haunted her during the day like a black dog on her trail. She couldn't escape them.

As a child, Ingrid's father had told her that it was important to have a vision and dream for the future. He said that it was extremely important to never give up and to always keep dreams and hopes alive. She could still hear his voice as he would say, “Sunshine, never, never lose your dreams. Your dreams today will be your realities tomorrow.”

She wanted to scream out to her father, “How do I have a vision in this kind of place?” However, in the middle of the night, she would try to create a vision of her future that would sustain her until she was free. She remembered reading about the psychiatrist Viktor Frankl who wrote in his book *Man's Search for Meaning* how he had survived the holocaust by having a powerful vision of the future and a deep sense of meaning and purpose. Ingrid imagined herself sitting on the front porch of a house on a beach somewhere in the world. Beside her was John Martin, the love of her life, holding her hand. They were growing old together. Every time she closed her eyes, each time she had negative feelings or was depressed and ready to give up, she practiced imagining her future with John. So far, it has worked and helped her hold on to her sanity.

Around 2:00 am the next morning, she heard a gunshot and loud noises outside the prison. She heard someone screaming. “What's going on?” she asked the grumpy old guard who was walking by.

“Someone tried to escape, but they didn't get very far,” he said, “This prison has a new fence that is lethal. If you touch it one time, the electrical jolt will knock you back. If touched a second time, it will deliver 15,000 volts of electricity, and the victim dies a painful death.”

Ingrid turned over and tried to go back to sleep, but it was useless. She recalled when she was a little girl how she would wake up early and open her bedroom window. She would listen to the birds outside in the trees. In the prison, the only birds she heard or saw were vultures.

The prison was becoming unbearable. Lydia had been released the day before. According to the guards, the officials had decided that Lydia was not worth holding any longer so they told her they would take her to the Israeli border crossing and release her. Ingrid had told her before she left that if she could possibly get word to Fox, then Ingrid might get released. Ingrid has promised Lydia a handsome reward if she was released. Ingrid hoped and prayed that Lydia would be able to get the message to Fox if she made it back to her homeland.

Ingrid later learned from one of the guards that Lydia was part of a prisoner exchange deal worked out between Israel and Syria. She had been selected in order to obtain the number of Israelis released in exchange for two terrorists held in an Israeli prison near Jericho. The guard had laughed when telling this to Ingrid, and said, “She was worthless to us.”

A few hours later, Ingrid heard the guard coming down the hall and was startled out of her daydreaming about food. The guard was escorting a short woman dressed in traditional Arab clothing down the hall. He stopped in front of Ingrid's cell, inserted the key, and opened the door. He pushed the woman inside and told Ingrid that she should enjoy the woman's company since she was also a spy.

Ingrid noticed immediately that the woman seemed to have a bad attitude. She plopped down her few meager belongings on Ingrid's lower bunk. Ingrid looked at her and said, “That is my bed.” The woman pushed her things to one end and lay down on the bed. Ingrid said again in a firmer voice, “That is my bed.”

The woman didn't move, so Ingrid grabbed her arm and pulled her off the bed. She landed on the floor with a thud. The woman jumped up and started swinging her fists, and they were immediately engaged in a fistfight, and hair-pulling contest.

The guard, still being somewhat close by, heard the noise and ran back to the cell yelling, “What’s going on here?” He grabbed Ingrid's arms and pulled her away from the other woman. He slammed her against the wall, sending a jarring pain through her back.

After calming down a bit, Ingrid realized that the best thing to do would be to move to the top bunk and try to get along with the woman. Ingrid looked at the woman and said in broken Arabic, "You can have this bed. I'll take the top." The woman watched Ingrid with a look of distrust.

CHAPTER 18 – John

John was rushing through the Atlanta airport when he heard the announcer's final boarding call for flights to Denver. He arrived, breathless, at the designated gate, presented his boarding pass, and hurried onto the plane. He found his seat and sat down as the plane's door was being closed.

He took a deep breath, thinking how close he had come to spending another night away from home. His flight from Argentina had arrived late. John began to think about how the hectic pace was getting old and wondering how much longer he could keep it up. He closed his eyes and let his thoughts drift to Ingrid. He tended to think of her any time he had a quiet moment. He was still haunted by her and struggled with a deep-rooted feeling that he had missed something when he had searched for her in Jordan. In his heart, he had never accepted the story he had been told about her death. But how would he ever find out, and where would he start looking? It was difficult to figure out when he had nothing to go on.

He felt a constant gnawing ache inside that wouldn't go away, and he often found it hard to concentrate on work. It was like an all-consuming fire that kept him from being his best. He didn't want to talk to anyone and didn't want anyone to talk to him. Yet he was so lonely inside and wanted to scream. "God, where are You?" he often asked. In the long hours of the night, he would cry out and wonder if God was listening. Night was the worst time to endure - waiting, hoping, praying – and he could hardly wait for daylight when he could once again lose himself in work. It was a two-edged sword. He had become more of a workaholic than ever to avoid thinking and hurting. He was exhausted from all the work and time on the road.

Early the next morning, at home in the Rockies, John got up and loaded the dogs in the Jeep. This time, he was not heading to Denver. Instead, he was heading deep into Estes Park. He had a knapsack with some lunch, and he was headed into the park to explore the trails. Winter would be arriving in a few weeks, and the high mountain peaks were covered with new snow. Soon, every trail would be covered in a blanket of white.

The dogs jumped out as John opened the door. They enjoyed the outdoors as much as he did. They spent the day in the mountains enjoying the last of fall's red and gold colors. They returned home when the shadows of night were creeping over the mountains like a veil.

John fell asleep with a prayer on his lips. "Oh God, if she is alive, please help me to find a way to get to her." He dreamed of sitting on the porch of a beach house holding her hand as they rocked back and forth watching the sunset. When he woke the next morning, he wondered if the dream was a sign. He was afraid to hope, afraid to dream, and afraid not to keep hoping. The anguish he felt was hard to describe and harder to make sense of. Only someone who had experienced the same kind of loss could understand the pain.

John decided it was time to call his old therapist friend, Joe Montgomery. Joe was a licensed family therapist and a long-time friend. They had worked together on a couple of assignments in years past. Joe was willing to make time to see John right away, so they agreed upon a time the next morning. John wasn't sure what he would say or how he would start, but he knew that he couldn't keep struggling with his feelings on his own.

At 10:00 am the next morning, John arrived at Joe's office. Joe looked at him in such a way that John felt that he was looking into his soul.

"Old friend, share with me what's going on in your world," he said. For the next hour, John poured out his heart and filled him in on the last few months. John saw a look of pain in his eyes as he listened to John's description of what he had learned about Ingrid's death.

John knew that Joe wouldn't be able to give definite answers, but he also knew that he would be able to help John look at various alternatives. Joe would also give John much needed support as he decided on a course to follow.

"Thanks, Joe," John said as he stood to leave at the end of the session. "I feel much better. It's so helpful to have someone to talk to."

"John, you can talk to me anytime you need to. Just let me know how you're doing," Joe said as they shook hands.

John drove home feeling a little better. At least he felt that he was not losing his mind. He was soon back home on the mountain, sitting by the fire, and trying to decide what to do about his course of action. He felt more and more that he had missed something in his search for Ingrid and that she was still alive somewhere in Jordan. He was deep in thought about how he could find her in such a hostile world. Even if she wasn't alive, he at least wanted to be able to bury her in her homeland. He made his decision – he must know for sure what has happened to her. He would go back to Jordan.

John called Ingrid's mother and told her of his

plans. “Oh, thank you, John. Thank you so much. I too believe that she is still alive. At night, it is as though I hear her voice calling out to me. Please find her if you can. I will be praying,” she said. “Please call me the minute you find out anything.” John assured her that he would call her no matter what he found out.

CHAPTER 19 - *Ingrid*

The days dragged by in the prison. There was little to do but think. Think about what might have been, think about family, and dream about John and what was most important in life. Each night after dark, Ingrid slipped off her cot and knelt to pray that God would sustain her and help her get home. She also prayed for her mother and sister and hoped that someday she would see them again. She still included Lydia in her prayers. If only she would let someone know that Ingrid was alive in this prison.

The guards seemed to be as miserable as the prisoners. They too were confined in the hot, miserable place. Ingrid tried to talk to them in Arabic, but they didn't have much to say. They knew little about what was going on in the outside world since they were at the low end of the food chain as far as the Syrian military was concerned. Ingrid prayed for them and found some peace in thinking of them as human beings with souls and not as animals like some of the prisoners referred to them.

Each morning, the prisoners were given a little bread and some rice and little else. During the remainder of the day, they were given little to eat. It is such a poor country, and they have little to eat by themselves. Ingrid longed for her home and the taste of a Belgium waffle, some chocolate, and a little pasta. She dreamed of home-cooked meals prepared by her mother. Her family didn't have an abundance of money, but they were fortunate enough to always have good food. Ingrid's mother believed in preparing healthy meals for her family.

Ingrid's new cellmate had calmed down some over time; however, she still didn't attempt to talk. Ingrid's feeble efforts to be kind to her had not paid off so far.

The woman seemed to be filled with hatred and an internal rage that was frightening. Ingrid had heard that she was reportedly a terrorist who had been captured getting on a bus with a backpack of explosives. The military had caught her by surprise and stripped the backpack away before she could detonate it; thus, interfering with her plans to take a shortcut to heaven, according to what she had been taught.

Ingrid was taken into the interrogation room once again. The room was almost dark – no windows and only a single light hanging from the ceiling by its wire. Jamul returned and impatiently began to yell at her.

"Who is your contact?" he demanded. "Why were you taking pictures of the terrorist camp in Petra?"

He seemed dissatisfied with every response Ingrid gave him. She patiently explained that she was only a reporter and that the pictures were taken by her cameraman, David Friedman. Ingrid told him that she didn't know where David was.

Jamul hammered her with questions for over an hour. Finally, he slammed his fist on the table and yelled," OK, we have ways to make you talk." He left the room.

A few minutes later, he returned. He grabbed Ingrid's arm and pulled her down the hall to another room. Her heart sank as she entered the room. It appeared to be a torture chamber. It reminded her of something that she had seen in a movie as a child. Jamul strapped Ingrid into a straight back wooden chair, slapped her with the back of his hand, and said, "You will talk now. You will tell us the truth."

Another man entered the room. Ingrid spotted the syringe he was carrying. He grabbed her hand and inserted the needle. She screamed in pain.

Almost immediately, her brain started to feel foggy. She was no longer sure where she was or what she was saying. She felt confused. She could hear the interrogators' questions, but she wasn't aware of whether she was saying anything or what she might be saying.

Ingrid slowly awakened to find that she was back in her cell. She was guessing that several hours had passed because she was terribly hungry and thought that even the poor food served to the prisoners would taste good at that point. She tried to remember what had transpired in the interrogation room, but the last thing she remembered was seeing the large needle and feeling the pain.

> *I remember a similar pain when I was a child. I was climbing a tree playing with Rebecca. We often played in the park a few blocks down from our flat. There was a large oak tree that I loved to climb and hide in. I could hear my sister calling for me and trying to find where I was hiding. I climbed as high as I could go and got lost in the branches. It was a beautiful warm spring Saturday. I decided to lie back and wait for her to find me. I thought I would close my eyes for a few minutes and rest from the climb.*
>
> *The next thing I knew, it was getting dark. My sister had obviously given up looking for me long ago and had walked home without me. I knew my mum would be angry with me for being gone so long. I hurriedly climbed down from the tree*

> *and somehow my foot slipped on the big branch a few feet from the ground. The next thing I knew, I was lying on the ground in severe pain. My arm was aching. I tried to scream, but no sound came out of my mouth. I looked around for someone to help me, but the park was deserted.*

Ingrid had managed to get to her feet and walk home, crying every step of the way. Her mother, who was standing at the open kitchen window, heard her crying as she neared home. She hurried outside to see what was wrong.

Her mom had looked at her arm and immediately called for Ingrid's father. They had carried her to the car and taken her to Dr. Mueller. Her arm was broken. The pain subsided after a while from the medication the doctor had given her, and they left his office with her arm in a white plaster cast.

Ingrid remembered that when they returned home, she was so hungry she was willing to eat anything. Her mother had been preparing dinner before the excitement, so she had finished the preparations and in a few minutes the table was set with fresh bread, pasta covered with hamburger and Ingrid's favorite garlic flavored sauce. Ingrid could still smell that meal. She had eaten so much that night that her stomach hurt.

The cast had been her burden for the rest of that summer. She had gotten it off in time for soccer practice in the fall. When the cast was removed, her left arm looked so white and small compared to her other arm, it had been weak for some time afterwards. Rebecca often challenged her later to climb the old oak tree again, but Ingrid had decided that her tree climbing days were over.

Ingrid was startled back into reality when the guard brought a tray with some bread and thin potato soup. Ingrid looked at the food and tried to pretend it was her mother's homemade vegetable soup and quickly consumed it.

The next day, Jamul walked by and laughed at her saying, "You tell us plenty. You are a big spy. We will have another talk with you soon."

Days passed and they didn't attempt to question her again. Ingrid hoped that they believed she had been telling the truth, but she was concerned that they still might not let her go free. She felt like her life was slipping away, and she had no hope of escape. She tried to keep a positive outlook for the future, but it had become increasingly difficult to do so. Some days, she found herself slipping into depression. She would try to pull herself back by imagining scenes on the beach with John holding her hand. Someday, she thought, someday.

CHAPTER 20 - John

John's plane was sitting on a runway waiting to take off for the Middle East. He closed his eyes and whispered a prayer. "Oh God, please lead me to where Ingrid is. And if she's still alive, please help me to get there in time."

As he was finishing the prayer, the plane's captain said that they were finally ready for takeoff. John looked around him and saw that the plane leaving Denver was full, as usual.

The plane rumbled down the runway, and John was once again amazed that such a massive object could fly. As they rose into the air, the plane shuddered as it balanced its heavy load and climbed toward a cruising altitude of 38,000 feet. John sat back and closed his eyes. He often fell asleep in the first few minutes of a flight, but not today. Today, he couldn't stop thinking about Ingrid and the possibility that she might be alive in some horrible situation in Jordan. He tried to think about sitting with Ingrid on the front porch of their home or on a beach someplace in the world, listening to the rush of waves.

> *My mind wanders back to a time when I was about 10-years old. My father and I often drove through the mountains exploring. We would occasionally stumble upon some ghost town and wander around trying to imagine what it had been like in its heyday. On this day, however, we drove on what appeared to be a deserted mountain trail. As we climbed higher and higher in the mountains, we were amazed at the beauty all around. We saw herds of mule deer grazing in the*

meadows. Once we saw a grizzly bear amble across the road in front of us. "What a beautiful place," my father commented. I sat spellbound at the abundance of wildlife we were seeing. Off in the distance, I thought I saw something lying on a large boulder. When I looked through my binoculars, I realized that it was a mountain lion sunning itself in the afternoon warmth. Soon, we rounded a curve in the trail and came to an old cabin. At first, we thought it was abandoned and then we heard a dog barking. I noticed someone sitting on the front porch in a rocking chair. As we drew closer, I noticed two people rocking and holding hands. We pulled up close and stopped. My dad turned off the engine and said, "Hello there. This sure is a beautiful country."

"Thanks," the old timer said. "We like it here. My wife and I have been here for over 12 years now." My dad said, "Well, you live in a beautiful place."

"Come in and have a cup of coffee," the lady said.

"Thanks. That would be nice. We have wandered quite a few miles away from home."

As we walked onto the old wooden porch, the old timer motioned to a couple of chairs off to the right. We walked over and sat down. His wife got up and headed into the house.

"We retired here several years

ago," the old timer began. "I worked in construction for many years, traveled over much of the world, grew tired of the rat race, and came here to find some peace and quiet," he continued. "By the way, my name is Howard Dove. Folks call me "Hoot." And this is my wife Marie."

"My name is Jerry Martin, and this is my son, John," my dad replied.

While they talked, I sat spellbound, looking at the beautiful sights around the old cabin. Off to the left on a small hillside, I saw several apple trees. And beyond that, I noticed what looked like a small vineyard. The grapes were glistening in the sun as they hung from the vines.

Soon, Marie came out with three cups of coffee and a large glass of lemonade for me. It seemed as though the adults talked for hours. I wandered off to play with their dog "Bullet." I threw a stick, and he chased it and brought it back to me repeatedly. Hoot gave my dad and me a tour of the cabin, and we were amazed at the simple way this couple lived. "We have no electricity here," Hoot said. "We use candles and a few oil lanterns to see at night. We listen to the news on a battery-powered radio. We have a rock cellar to store our food in, and we have a refrigerator run by propane gas, so we have all the comforts we need."

Wow, I thought, they don't even have TV. How can anyone live without TV?

The sun was sinking over the

horizon when my dad said, "Thanks so much for your hospitality, but John and I must be going. I can't tell you how much we've enjoyed visiting with you folks."

"Come again any time," Hoot said. "We always enjoy company."

"Yes. Come back and bring your wife with you next time," Marie said. My dad lowered his head and said slowly, "My wife passed away last year. But John and I would love to come back and visit with you sometime soon."

"Please do," they said. We got in the car and started off down the trail. I looked back and waved, and I saw them sitting on the porch holding hands again as the sun was setting in the western sky.

Someone was shaking John's arm. "Excuse me, sir," the lady sitting in the seat beside him was saying. "I need to get by you to go to the restroom."

"Sure. I guess I was daydreaming," said John.

John sat back down thinking about Hoot and Marie holding hands on the porch of that old cabin and thought that it was one of the most beautiful sights he had ever seen. He had wished he could have seen his parents doing that but since his mom had died, it had been so lonely.

He wondered what had happened to Hoot and Marie. He and his dad had talked about going back, but things had gotten busy for his dad and they never made the trip. John had always felt a pain of regret when remembering them. Someday, he would like to try to find out what happened to them.

John was jolted back to reality when the airplane hit turbulence. The pilot came on and warned the passengers to remain seated while he tried to find smoother flying at a higher altitude.

This flight was long, and John was finding it difficult to get comfortable and rest. He took out his laptop and pulled up a map of Jordan on the internet. He was at a loss as to where to begin looking for Ingrid. He had decided before leaving Denver that he needed to hire a guide who was trustworthy. He had contacted the American embassy, and they had provided him with three names as candidates. The first one he contacted was not available on the dates John would need him. The next one had refused to take the assignment saying simply that it was too dangerous to be around Petra. Finally, for a hefty fee, the third one had agreed to meet John at his hotel in Amman. However, he had stated very firmly, "We must talk first. Then I will let you know if I will do it."

John dozed off after dinner and dreamed again – the same dream about the house on the beach. This time, however, the dream seemed even more real. The setting was like a town near Riga, Latvia, a place John had visited several years earlier. It was a lovely little resort town that was used by the communist government officials as a vacation getaway when Latvia had been part of the old Soviet Union. Now, the town was a beautiful quaint community on the Baltic Sea.

He woke with the dream fresh in his mind. He thought about what a great place it would be to retire and live. The town and beach along the Baltic Sea was beautiful. It had old homes that were constantly being restored and modernized. He thought about a carving he had at home that he had bought on his last trip to the area.

The shop merchant had told him that the artist who made it was unable to work anymore due to his severe alcoholic condition. This was not unusual in the old Soviet Union. So many of the men there drank vodka like Americans drink soft drinks. In Latvia, many women were widowed by middle age because so many men died young due to alcoholism. Latvia was struggling to recover from its years of communist domination. John recalled walking into an old Greek Orthodox Church while a funeral had been in progress. He stood off to one side and observed. The coffin had been like those used in the old west over a hundred years ago. They were small and made of wood, with the entire body visible. The women attending the funeral wore headscarves and stood over one elderly lady, praying softly. John had slipped out the side door without being noticed. Further down the street from the church was a beautiful castle that was over three hundred years old. Under the communist regime, it had deteriorated and was crumbling. It was such a tragedy to see a country's deterioration because of the corruption and greed of officials robbing the country for their own profit. The people were poor and had little healthy food, but they were some of the nicest, warmest people John had met in his travels all over the world.

John thought that if he could find Ingrid, perhaps one day they could live and retire on the Baltic Sea far away from the hurried pace of the U.S., Europe, and other major parts of the world. He prayed again that she was alive and that he would be able to find her soon. The pilot announced that they had been cleared to land in Amman.

John sat up and braced himself for what might be the most difficult task of his life.

CHAPTER 21 - Lydia

Lydia was back in Jerusalem. She was on a frantic search to find where her children had been taken. She went to the state-run orphanage and asked questions, but no one there had seen them. She wandered the streets in her old neighborhood asking her former neighbors about them, but no one seemed to know anything about them.

Her uncle and his wife had taken her in when she returned, and they attempted to help her regain her sanity. She was constantly talking, but her words made no sense to them. Her uncle worked at the local diamond market where tourists came to buy gems at cheaper prices than in many countries. He was engrossed in his business and unwilling to devote time to aid her in her search.

Each day, she walked the streets looking, asking, and crying. Several weeks had passed now, and she'd had no success. Her heart was breaking. She had lost everything in her life that had been dear to her. She wandered aimlessly through the streets of old Jerusalem, bumping into tourists, and chasing down children at play hoping that one of them would be hers. She went into one of the many churches and found a seat in the back. The church was located near the pool of Salome where the poor and injured came to be placed in the water. The church was known for having the most perfect acoustics of any other church in Jerusalem. Lydia was hoping that she too could find healing here.

After sitting and praying for hours she walked outside and went to the merchant who sold fresh fruit near the Muslim quarter of the old city. When she walked up to gaze at the baskets of fruit, she remembered that she had been to the shop before. The shopkeeper saw her and slowly approached her and said, "Lydia? Is that you? It cannot be."

"Yes," she replied. "Do you remember me? Have you seen my children?"

Slowly he approached her to make sure that it was her. He couldn't believe the change in her appearance since the last time he had seen her. "Yes," he whispered, "I have seen your children. They have been cared for by your cousin. They attend a school not far from here."

"Where?" she pleaded. "Where is the school?"

He walked to the back of the shop and spoke to his wife to tell her he would return soon. "Come, Lydia. I will show you," he said.

With tears running down her cheeks, she said, "Thank you, thank you, thank you."

"Lydia," he gently said, "you must tell me what has happened to you, and where you have been for the past years."

"I will tell you everything, but first I must see my children," she said.

When they arrived at the school, the shopkeeper walked inside ahead of Lydia so that her appearance wouldn't frighten the teachers and students. He spoke to the head teacher, and she gazed long and hard at Lydia. "Are you sure she is the children's mother?" she asked.

"Yes. I grew up with her husband, and they have been to my shop many times. Her name is Lydia," he replied.

The teacher asked them to wait while she went to get the children from their classrooms. When they appeared in the hallway, Lydia began to cry again. As they approached her, she knelt and opened her arms to them. The children approached cautiously, unsure who this woman was that was crying and reaching for them. They looked at her for a long moment and gradually moved a little closer.

The shopkeeper knelt beside them and whispered to them, “This is your mama.”

“No, it cannot be," the older child said. "Our mama and papa are dead. They were killed.”

Lydia responded, “No, your papa is dead, but I survived, and I’m here to take you home with me.” They recognized her voice and walked closer. She pulled them to her side and began to kiss them and tell them how much she loved them.

Lydia thanked the shopkeeper again and walked with her children through the cobblestone streets to where her cousin lived. When they entered the small apartment over one of the many souvenir shops, the children raced ahead up the stone stairs and called out, “Mama is here! Mama is here!"

Lydia’s cousin Ruth was in the kitchen where delicious aromas of freshly baked bread and stew wafted through the door. Ruth looked at Lydia. “Is it really you?”

Lydia, once again in tears, said, “Yes, Ruth. It's me. I’m so glad to see you and thank you for taking care of my children.”

“Come. Sit down and tell me where you have been. We thought you were dead,” Ruth said in a trembling voice. Ruth led her to a wooden chair at the small table near the window. A gentle breeze was coming through the window causing the old ragged curtains to float in the air. Lydia sat down and the children sat near her at her feet. It was as though they didn't want to leave her side for fear of being separated again. Slowly, Lydia began to recount the story of the time when she and her husband were traveling near the border of Syria. She told how they got lost and were captured. With a sob in her voice she looked into her children's eyes and told them how much their father loved them, and then she told them of his death. Everyone cried as she told them of her years in prison and her longing for them.

As she neared the end of her story, she suddenly remembered Ingrid and her words, "Please call Fox and tell them I am here and tell them I am alive."

"Oh, Ruth!" she blurted. "In my grief, I forgot to tell you about my cellmate in that horrible place. She was a beautiful young woman from Europe. I can't remember where, but that is not important," she continued. "Her name is Ingrid, and she was a reporter. I think she said she worked for Fox... no, no, that isn't right. It was CNN. I need to get word to them that she is still alive. I promised her that I would try to help her."

"Oh, Lydia," Ruth interrupted. I'm not so sure that would be a good idea. If you get involved with the terrorist prison camps, those people may come after you and harm you or the children. You know how they are, and you know that they have many friends and supporters in Palestine."

"I never thought about that," Lydia replied. "You could be right. Yet, I did promise to try to help her. But I can't risk losing my children again."

Ruth reminded her of the terror that is a constant presence in Israel. "We must be cautious and do nothing to bring attention to ourselves," Ruth continued.

Lydia was so joyful at finding her children that she soon forgot about her promise to Ingrid. "God will forgive me," she told herself. She and the children decided to continue living with Ruth so that the children could remain in their current school.

CHAPTER 22 – John & Ishmael

John's cab pulled up in front of the same hotel he had stayed in when he first arrived in Amman. The cab stopped at the bottom of the steps of the hotel for him to get out. The hotel was located on a hillside overlooking the city. Even though the hotel was beautiful architecturally, it held no fond memories for John. When he had left a few months earlier he felt as low as he had ever felt. As usual after international flights, John was tired and suffering from jet lag because of the 10-hour time difference. It wasn't unusual for his feet to swell after a long flight, and he noticed them as he climbed the steps leading to the entrance of the hotel. When he entered the lobby, a strong feeling of loneliness swept over him, and he wanted to run away. He willed himself to walk to the front desk and check in. He went to his room and fell across the bed, exhausted. Sometime later, he woke and realized that he hadn't undressed before falling asleep. At 10:00 am, he was in the lobby ready to meet the potential guide. He selected a seat that allowed him full view of the hotel entrance.

After waiting for more than an hour, a man walked in and seemed to be searching for someone. John heard him ask the desk clerk for John and saw her point in his direction as he stood up and started toward the man. He had a large smile and called to John in broken English as he approached. He introduced himself as Ishmael, and John reached out and they shook hands. He began to talk rapidly, and John had trouble understanding him. “Can you please slow down?" John asked, "so, I can better understand you.”

“I'm so sorry,” said Ishmael, and he continued more slowly by asking where John thought the lady he was searching for might be located.

John shared with him the details of his last search and noticed Ishmael 's face growing grimmer by the moment. When John finished, Ishmael was shaking his head. He said to John, "Those are bad men near Petra, very bad men."

"Will you please help me," John pleaded. "I need someone to guide me." They discussed payment. Now that he knew more details, Ishmael wanted twice as much as the amount they had originally discussed. He told John his fee would be $1,000 per week. They finally agreed on $700 per week, and John headed upstairs to get his bags so they could get started.

They loaded John's bags into the back of Ishmael 's small car and headed to the rental car agency. John rented a Land Rover that would give them plenty of room to store the supplies they would need for several days in the wilderness. After stocking up on provisions, they headed off in the direction of Petra. They planned to begin by carefully backtracking from the small town where the large black Mercedes had stopped John on his last quest when the men told him that Ingrid was dead.

They interviewed several people the guide knew but learned very little new information. Since several months had passed, no one remembered seeing the car.

They continued through the desert. The temperature was well over 100°F. John wiped the sweat from his face frequently. They didn't use the air conditioning except in the hottest part of the day because using it caused the car to use more gas, and the price of gas was extremely high. Also, there was a long distance between gas stations.

They drove until after dark and finally stopped and

unrolled sleeping bags in the back of the Land Rover since there were no hotels. They were trying to figure out the location where Ingrid's accident had taken place. They asked everyone they encountered along the way if they remembered an accident in which a young woman had been killed or seriously injured.

They woke at sunup and rolled up the sleeping bags. They had a quick breakfast of granola bars and bottled water as they continued their journey. Around midday, they saw a small boy and his father tending some sheep near a small stream. They stopped, and Ishmael walked towards the boy. John reached into a bag in the back of the car and grabbed a candy bar. When John walked over to them, Ishmael was talking to the boy in Arabic and his father was hurrying over to where they stood. The boy nodded his head and said, "Yes, I remember such an accident." As the boy's father walked up, he quickly told the boy to stop talking. As the boy stepped behind his father, John handed him the candy bar which he took reluctantly.

"We know nothing about such an accident," the man said. "The boy is mistaken."

Ishmael reached into his pocket and took out the equivalent of $5 and held it out to the man. "Are you sure? It was a green Land Rover."

The man reached out and took the money and stuffed it in his pocket. "Oh yes. Now that you mention the color, I think I do remember. It was several kilometers from here," pointing back in the direction from which we had just come.

"Would you show us?" Ishmael asked.

The man shook his head no, until John reached into his pocket and pulled out the equivalent of $10 and handed it to him. Slowly he and the boy climbed into the back of the Land Rover, and Ishmael turned the vehicle around and headed back. After traveling for about fifteen minutes, the man told him to stop. He got out and walked slowly down the road to the south, then slowly back to the north, going a good distance away from the vehicle. Finally, he waved his hands and yelled, "This is the place."

They drove to where he stood and pulled to the side of the road. They looked around, and the man pointed to a large boulder on the side of the road. John was surprised as he looked and saw green paint on the side of the rock. Ishmael and John started walking into the desert on both sides of the road looking for any clues. John saw something tan, almost the color of the desert sand, snagged in a small bush. He walked over and picked it up. It was a piece of seatbelt. His heart skipped several beats when he looked closer at it and noticed that it looked like it had been cut with a knife. He recalled that when he had looked at the wrecked Land Rover, part of the driver's seatbelt was missing.

"Ishmael. Look at this. It has been cut with a knife." Ishmael examined it and agreed. They found no other evidence, but then the constant shifting of the desert sands could have covered anything over in the months since the accident. The man told Ishmael that he had heard that a foreign woman had been seen with a band of Bedouins, but he didn't know where they might be camped now.

Ishmael looked at John and started to shake his head. "This is very bad news. If the Bedouins have her, they will keep her as a slave wife, trade her to another tribe, or kill her if she causes them too much trouble." He continued, "There is no law in their tribes except their own law, and it is very harsh."

As perspiration rolled down John cheeks like

tears, he thought that if this was true, then it would be very difficult, if not impossible, to find Ingrid. The thoughts of what might have happened to her dampened the good news that she had probably survived the accident. After all, John thought, there couldn't be many foreign women with the Bedouins.

They took the man and boy back to the spot where they had left their sheep and then drove back to the site of the accident. This would become the central focus of their search. From here, they would drive in several directions to look for other clues about where the Bedouins might have gone. It was almost dark, so they rolled out their sleeping bags and slept under the stars. As John was looking into the night sky and stars overhead, he whispered a prayer. “Dear God, please help us find her. Please guide us to look in the right direction.” He closed his eyes and listened to Ishmael's snores as he fell asleep.

CHAPTER 23 - Ingrid

Things had been quiet in the prison for a few days. Ingrid had not been interrogated, beaten, or drugged again. The guards seemed preoccupied with other prisoners. As Ingrid reflected on these thoughts, she whispered, "Thank you, God. Thank you that I am still alive, and please let John and I be together again someday."

She thought about how many exciting news events had taken place since she had been imprisoned, and she felt a surge of regret that she had missed them. As she lay on her bunk looking at the ceiling, she wondered what had been happening between the Palestinians and Israelis.

Her mind wandered to something her mother had told her the last time they had been together. Ingrid had thought about that night so many times, and she was still shaken by the family secret that her mother shared with her that night.

> *My mum took my hand, and I saw a tear in her eye, when she said "Ingrid, there is something I learned recently that I want to share with you. Just before my mum died, your grandmother, she called me to her bedside and confided some shocking information to me. She told me that near the end of World War II, she met a young American soldier. He was a paratrooper who came to Belgium to fight against the Germans. His platoon landed in a field near Luxembourg and marched to Bastonia where she and her parents lived. They set up a bivouac at the edge of town, preparing to defend the area in the Battle of the Bulge. It was a bitterly*

cold winter, and many of the local families were kind to the troops. Many were invited to spend time in the homes of the citizens. There they were given hot food and warm beds to sleep in.

Her parents had invited a young officer named James Rubin from Alabama to stay with them. Young Sgt. Rubin was so kind and was obviously very worried about the coming battle. He would sit and talk with her father for hours at night. They had prepared a room for him on the third floor of our old farmhouse, and the rest of the family slept on the second floor. She told me that she was very attracted to him and that she would heat bricks each night in the fireplace and place them in his bed to keep his feet warm. He had suffered some minor frostbite, and his feet hurt quite a bit.

He was with them for several weeks. He began to pay special attention to your grandmother. They were close in age. After he had stayed with them for several days, she would wait until everyone was asleep at night and slip up to his room and sit on the floor by his bed and ask him questions about his life in America. He had been raised in a small town called Chattanooga, Tennessee, and spent a lot of his childhood on the Tennessee River. He talked about loving to fish with his father and younger brother and how much he missed them. She said she could feel the love for his family through his words.

She said he was especially lonely and sad as Christmas 1944 grew closer. One night, he slipped his hand over hers, and began to hold her hand and look into her eyes and talk about how much he loved talking with her. On Christmas night, she gave him a gift that she had made for him. She had taken his old sleeping bag and sewn the inside with her fur coat so that he would be warm at night when he was sleeping in the foxholes in the snow. She also took an old bed sheet and made him a camouflage garment that he could wear over his fatigues so that he would not be so visible in the snow. He gave her his high school class ring and asked her to wait for him until after the war.

They began to kiss and became more excited. She said that before she realized what she was doing, she had slipped into his bed. He began to run his hands over her, and they became more excited. After that night, she would slip up to his room each night until his platoon was shipped out in the middle of January. He promised her he would come back to her after the war. He wanted to take her to America with him and promised to build them a home on the Tennessee River.

Weeks went by and the fighting became vicious. Finally, the Germans were driven back into Germany and the war ended soon thereafter. She realized in March that she was pregnant. This was a huge dilemma. She was going to have a baby and she was only 19 years old and not married. She heard nothing from him for several months. Finally, as the war ended, she received a letter from his commanding officer. The letter indicated that a German Panzer unit had broken through the line he was defending during battle, and he had been wounded. One of his men carried him to the medic station. Captain Johnson, who sent the letter, went there to visit Sgt. Rubin, who begged the captain to get in touch with the woman he loved to let her know of his injuries and where he was located. Captain Johnson assured him he would let her know, and in the middle of the night, Sgt. Rubin died.

After the war, your grandmother's childhood sweetheart came to visit her after he was released from an occupation camp. Once he learned of her situation, he offered to marry her. He said he had always loved her and that he would raise the child as his own. Ingrid, the man you knew as your grandfather was not really your grandfather. Your grandfather was an American. He was buried near the battlefield. General Eisenhower had troops who were killed during the war buried near the battlefield with a wooden cross to mark the location. Since Sgt. Rubin never left Europe, his family never knew that he had a child. I wanted to let them know, but it was too complicated. Soon after your grandmother told me this story, she died. Now I don't know what to do. So many years have passed, and I don't know if I should try to get to know my real father's family.

My mum started to cry, and I wrapped my arms around her. I thought you should know, especially since you have fallen in love with an American. You may go to America someday and want to find them. With that, she handed me a piece of paper with the name and address of my real grandfather written on it. I stored the address in my computer and saved the piece of paper with my jewelry.

Now, as Ingrid thought about what her mother had told her, she longed even more to get out of the prison. There were so many things she wanted to do with her life. "Dear God, deliver me from this place," she prayed. Then she rolled over with her face to the wall and cried.

CHAPTER 24 – JOHN & ISHMAEL

They woke up as the sun peeped over the horizon. They were planning to pick up where we had left off the day before. They had few clues to follow as they drove through the desert. The sun was intense as they stopped to examine a heap of stones piled up in one spot. Ishmael said, "This is the grave of a Bedouin woman."

"How can you tell?" asked John.

"There is no tombstone, which means that she was a young Bedouin bride who was not a virgin on her wedding night. She dishonored her family, and her father would have killed her. It is their way."

"A father would kill his own daughter?" John whispered. "How could a father kill his own flesh and blood?"

"If she does not prove to be a virgin on her wedding night, her husband will tell the father. The father must kill her for dishonoring his family. The husband can then select another young bride," he continued.

John was horrified and said as much to Ishmael, who shrugged and said, "It is their way."

Later that day, they came to a small village. The children were playing in the middle of the main road. As soon as they saw the strangers, they ran to the side of the road and picked up trinkets to try to sell to them. They ran up to the side of the vehicle and pounded on the doors and windows on both sides. "One dollar," they yelled repeatedly. "One dollar, mister," they said as they shook a useless trinket in front of our faces hoping that we would buy it. John and Ishmael shook their heads and said, "No, no." The children didn't give up. The vehicle rolled to a stop at a building that looked like it might be a hotel and possibly a restaurant. As they got out, Ishmael said in Arabic, “No, no. Go away. We will not buy it.” Then he looked at John and said, “Do not buy anything. If you do, the others will not leave you alone until you buy from them. They are very persistent."

Many of the poor areas of the world are filled with children begging in much the same way. John always felt heartbroken over so much poverty.

They walked into the hotel. John glanced around and saw two old men sitting at a table in the corner playing a game that reminded him of checkers. They stopped their game and looked at the two new arrivals. Ishmael talked to the woman behind the desk, “Do you have rooms and food?” he asked as he pulled out Euros from his shirt pocket. “Yes,” she answered in her native tongue. She indicated the price, Ishmael paid her, and she led them upstairs to two small rooms at the end of the hall. John looked around. They were in a small room containing a small bed, a toilet, and a wash basin. No TV, no phone, and certainly none of the comforts of even a cheap hotel in America would be found here.

Ishmael went back to the Land Rover to get their bags and carried them inside. He knocked on John's door. When John opened the door, Ishmael said, "Be very careful. Do not leave any valuables in this room. The people here are very poor as you can see. They will take anything they can find if they think they can sell it.”

Ishmael closed the door and walked to his room. John’s mind drifted back to the stone grave and wondered how a father could ever bring himself to kill his own daughter. This culture was totally foreign to him. He had witnessed the pain American parents had experienced at the loss of a child. He knew that many of those families were permanently torn apart because they were unable to deal with the pain. He could not fathom what the pain of killing your own child would be like or how anyone could deliberately do such a horrible thing.

There was pounding on his door, and John realized that he had lost track of time. Ishmael called out to him that it was time for dinner. John opened the door and said, “Please give me a minute.” He went to the wash basin and splashed some cold water in his face. He knew the water was unsafe to drink.

As they sat down to have dinner, Ishmael picked up a newspaper and started reading the headlines. "The presidential race in the U.S. isn't over,” he translated. “The candidates seem to be attacking each other on every front,” he said. “Your elections in America are sounding more and more like the elections in the rest of the world. The parties don’t trust each other anymore. They are not counting votes properly and have problems with allowing people to vote. What is happening to your country?”

John looked at him a few minutes before responding, “Maybe it's been going on all along and people are finally speaking out about it. I really don’t know,” he responded with a sigh.

Ishmael looked at him and said, “If we are to build a democracy like you have in America, then how do we avoid this kind of problem?”

“That, my friend, is a very good question,” John responded and looked up to see a plate of food being placed in front of him.

John bowed his head and whispered a prayer of thanks. When he looked up again, Ishmael was watching him. “You are a religious man, yes?” he questioned.

“Yes, I have a strong faith in God. And I believe He will use you to lead me to Ingrid.”

"Ah, Mr. John, I hope you are right. I too pray that Allah will lead us to your wife."

"Oh no," John explained. "Ingrid is not my wife, but I do love her and want her to become my wife after we find her."

Ishmael gazed out the window watching the scenes play out in the street for a long moment, then said, "We will try very hard to find her, but you must know it won't be easy, and it may take us a long time." They ate for a while before Ishmael continued. "I will walk around town and ask some questions. They won't talk if you are with me. You must wait here. I will return soon," he said as he finished his dinner and pushed his chair back and walked through the open door.

John tried to eat the remainder of his food which consisted of pita bread, humus, and meat. He was reluctant to ask what meat it was. It tasted a little like roast beef, but he knew it wasn't. At least it tasted better than some of the food he had eaten in some eastern European countries. It was better than the pork and cabbage that many of the people there so often ate. They made cabbage rolls with a little pork in them, and the smell alone is hard to take. John looked forward to when he could have American food again.

John recalled that he had visited a ranch in South Dakota once, where the cowboys prepared a traditional meal of steak, beans, and corn. Following the meal, they sang and played what they called real country music to the crowd with traditional western songs such as "Home on the Range" and "The Yellow Rose of Texas," followed by the reciting of Baxter Black poems. John wished he had brought his book of Baxter Black poetry with him. The poems always reminded him of home in Colorado. The radio in the rental vehicle was playing what was strange music to John, and he dozed off as they drove.

CHAPTER 25 – John & Ishmael

Ishmael shook John awake. He pointed off in the distance to his left. John stared into the sun and noticed a cloud of dust, an indication that a vehicle was approaching at a rapid speed. Ishmael slowed the rental and drove on as though he hadn't noticed. In a few minutes, the military-style truck pulled alongside them. The two men in the front seat were not dressed in military uniforms. Ishmael whispered, "They may be Hamas terrorists." The men looked at them closely as they passed and kept going. Ishmael followed behind at a safe distance and eventually lost sight of them as they continued in the direction of Petra.

As late afternoon approached, Ishmael told John that there was a tourist camp nearby where buses brought people to a Bedouin camp. The tourists were fed a meal of roasted lamb and typical Jordanian vegetables and rice. He suggested they stop there and have dinner. John agreed, and Ishmael pulled off to the right and told him that there were several such camps in the desert, especially in the Wadi rum area.

They stopped, and John gave money to a man in a white headdress for their meals. They were seated inside a tent on wooden benches at a table sitting atop beautiful Persian rugs. The tent cover was made in such a way as to keep some of the heat out. The lamb was roasted in a pit deep in the sand. It was some of the best tasting food John had ever eaten in this area of the world. After dinner, they continued toward Petra.

Late in the evening, they could see the rock mountain off to the right a few miles away. There was little vegetation to offer cover, so they stopped behind a rock formation to wait for darkness. They made a plan for entering the rock fortress and then took a nap for a couple of hours. Shortly after dark, they packed the few things they had lying around and started off with no lights on. As they neared the back side of the mountain, they slowed to a crawl until they found a rock overhang large enough to park the Land Rover under. Ishmael pulled the vehicle as far out of sight as possible, and they covered it with a desert camouflage tarp.

They took the rock-climbing equipment and started up the narrow path that led partway up the rock face. As they neared the end of the path, they began using the pickaxes and ropes to find footing to climb up further.

John wondered how Ingrid might be at that moment. "A risk-free life is a lonely life," he said to himself. There is no such thing as a risk-free relationship. He could only hope that the reward would be worth the risk and that he would find Ingrid. Ishmael looked at John with a questioning look. "Did you say something?" he asked.

"No," replied John. I must have been thinking out loud.

The sun was setting in the golden western sky when they approached the top of the large red rock mountain. Ishmael said, "This is the back side of Petra." They found an area where they could set up their tents and made camp for the night. They didn't build a fire in hope of going undetected.

John attempted to fall asleep, despite the emptiness he felt inside that had been with him since Ingrid had disappeared. The feeling seemed more intense than he had felt since the time of her disappearance. He pondered how relationships are difficult under the best of circumstances, but when love is lost it is one of the most gut-wrenching experiences in life. Yet when it is working, it is the most satisfying and fulfilling emotion a human can experience.

They woke early the next morning and began carefully exploring the area around Petra. It was challenging to find a place where they could enter without being detected. John wasn't sure they would find Ingrid here, but perhaps they would find a clue that would lead them to her. He felt certain that someone in Petra knew what had happened to Ingrid and David.

John thought, “What will I do if she is truly dead.” Then he remembered that he must force himself to control his negative thoughts.

Instead, he focused on his favorite scripture from the book of Romans, chapter 8, verse 28: *all things work together for good to them that love God, to them who are called according to his purpose.* "Well, Lord," he whispered, "I do believe that verse, but I sure wonder sometimes how anything good can come from some of life's painful experiences like the one I'm going through now."

They continued to carefully search for a way to get into Petra undetected. They knew that Hezbollah and Israel had been waging war in Lebanon and that any number of things could go wrong. John was convinced that he had to find Ingrid and get back to the beautiful Rocky Mountains before any more violence erupted in this area.

Ishmael said he had heard of an ancient pathway into the mountains, but he had never used it. He led John in the direction he recalled hearing about. They carefully edged their way around the rock mountain until they approached a cave-like entrance that was about two feet wide. They each squeezed into the entrance and found a crawlway. They had been on their hands and knees for thirty minutes when we saw sunshine again. They gradually came to an opening on the inside of Petra that was about fifty feet above the floor of the rock city. They used their ropes and lowered themselves to the floor. They were in a remote region near the back wall of the mountain. They found a place to hide and waited until dark.

As the sun set and darkness crept over the mountain, they left their hiding place and moved against the wall in the direction they thought would lead to the main entrance to the city. They came upon several portable trailers in the middle of the rock formations. They saw large drums inside the entrances to several of the buildings. They slipped inside one building and attempted to find out what was in the drums. Ishmael opened the one closest to him, and quickly dropped the lid back in place. He ran to the doorway gasping for air. He could hardly breathe and was speechless for several seconds. Gradually he whispered to John, "Chemical weapons. We have found a stockpile of chemical weapons probably belonging to the terrorists."

They worked their way over to the trailer in the rear of the group of trailers and tried the door. It was unlocked, so they went inside and turned on a flashlight from their small backpack. They saw computers and shelves of notebooks lining the walls. As they shone the small beam of light around them, they soon realized that all the equipment was used for training terrorists.

John took a deep breath and whispered, "Oh God, what have we found here?" He began to realize that Ingrid and David must have made the same discovery. He knew that the terrorists would not have let them live if they had discovered this place. Neither would they allow John and Ishmael to live if they were caught.

Hamas and Hezbollah had a cache of weapons here that could destroy several cities and kill and injure thousands of people. Ishmael attempted to get into one of the computers but was unable to. They unplugged it and slipped it into their backpack. As they were about to leave the trailer, John spotted a laptop case with Fox News on the outside. He grabbed it as they slipped out the door.

As they rounded a corner, they heard someone approaching. Two men were headed in their direction. They were talking softly, and one of them was smoking a cigarette. John and Ishmael crawled under the trailer and were barely out of sight when the two men walked by. They stopped near the door and looked around. John and Ishmael could hear their conversation, but only Ishmael could interpret what they were saying. John looked at him; his face was white as a sheet. He put his finger to his lips. John could understand a few words – Lebanon, Syria, Israel – but little else.

After a few minutes, the two men continued their patrol and moved out of sight. Ishmael motioned to John to follow him. They worked their way back to the rope they had left in place that would lead them up to the small crawlway that they had entered through. It was much more difficult to climb up in the dark than they had anticipated. It took them more than an hour to find the crawlway and get back to the outside.

Once out, they rushed back to their hidden

vehicle and started back to the hotel with no headlights on. John looked at Ishmael and asked, “What were they saying?”

He took a deep breath and began to fill John in on the conversation. It was about using weapons against the Israeli military. “They said that Syria is ready to use the weapons if the bombing of Lebanon resumes again,” he said. Ishmael looked at John who could see he was reluctant to continue.

“What else?” John asked.

He took another deep breath and sighed. “They said something about news reporters who gave away this location and that one is dead and the other must die.”

“Did they say which one is dead?” John asked quickly.

“No, but it was pretty clear that the one who must die is somewhere in Syria. They did not say where.”

“Then we must go to Syria,” John insisted.

Ishmael looked at him and said, “Syria is in the middle of civil war, it is very difficult to get into Syria, and it will be even more difficult to get out ... alive.”

John said, "I don’t care. We must try. If it's David who is still alive, he will be able to tell me what happened to Ingrid. And if she is the one still alive, then we must find a way to get her out of there."

Ishmael finally responded, "We will see if it is possible. First, we must get out of here. By the way, I found this small book inside the trailer and slipped it in my pocket. When we get to the hotel, I will try to translate it. It might provide some clues. It appears to be a diary."

They drove across the hot, dry desert as fast as they could safely go in the dark without headlights. They tried to stay on the same trail they had followed previously. Suddenly, Ishmael hit the brakes and they came to a sudden stop. The seatbelt jerked against John's shoulder. "What's going on?" he asked.

"I see lights ahead," Ishmael responded in a low voice. "They appear to be moving this way. It is possibly a patrol of some kind."

Ishmael pulled the Land Rover into a clump of low brush and stopped. He turned off the engine and sat still. They could tell that it was a fairly large truck and was heading quickly towards them. "If they see us, we could be in trouble," John said.

"You are right," said Ishmael, and he quickly climbed out the driver's side window to avoid a light coming on by opening the door. He went to the back of the vehicle and reached inside. He pulled out the camouflage tarp as John climbed out the window to help cover the vehicle. They crawled several yards away from the vehicle and hid in some rocks. They stayed silent while the truck approached.

They could hear voices coming from the truck. It appeared that they were not yet alarmed. The truck stopped about 100 meters from the covered Land Rover. One man got out and relieved himself. John and Ishmael could see in the glimmer of the moonlight that he was wearing a uniform. They could possibly be a patrol from the Jordanian army. They got back in the truck, and they sped away, passing within a few yards of John and Ishmael's hiding place.

They waited until the truck was out of sight and

they could no longer see its lights, and then slipped the tarp off the Land Rover and drove on.

Early the next morning, they arrived in a small village on their way to Amman. They found a small, ragged hotel, rented rooms, showered, and lay down for a few hours of much-needed sleep. John was awakened several hours later by Ishmael pounding on his door.

“We must go now,” he said in a low whisper when John opened the door. "I have not slept but have been translating the diary. You can drive while I tell you what it contains.”

John quickly grabbed his belongings, and they slipped down the back stairs to the Land Rover. John climbed in the driver's seat, and they drove away.

“Mister John,” Ishmael whispered, “we are in great danger. I overheard two men talking in the hotel.”

As John drove, Ishmael began to tell him what was in the diary. “This diary goes back over a long period of time. It is a record of daily activities of the group. It begins in the 1980s and tells of a plan to kill the Pope. The plan is to attempt to kidnap him and create a wax, life-size replica of him. This replica will be presented as his body. It will lie in state, and then be buried. People will believe it is the pope.”

“Why not just present the real body? And how do they plan to fool the world with a pile of wax?” John asked.

“That is the thing that is so surprising. There are several high-ranking Vatican officials who want this pope out of power. He is too conservative, and he is too influential. They don’t want him killed right away because he knows about secret documents hidden away that implicates them in a plot to overthrow him. They want him interrogated until he tells where the documents are hidden, then they want him killed, and his body destroyed.

John whispered, “What else does it say?”

"Many other things, but none of them will help us other than the last few entries. They offer some clues about the Fox News reporters.”

“What does it say about them?”

Ishmael paused. "It says that one of them was sent with a suicide terrorist and was killed in the attack. The other one is in a Syrian prison. It does not say which one. It indicates that the one in prison had a computer with pictures of Petra, and that they were obviously spies. It also indicates that orders have been given to kill the imprisoned spy.”

“Does it say when?” John asked.

“It does not say when, but it is a recent entry. I believe it will be soon.” he replied. "It also mentions that they believe there are more spies in the area. A military patrol reported finding strange tracks coming from Petra and headed this way,” Ishmael continued.

“Do they know we are here?” John asked.

Ishmael said, “No, they could not know. But they are certain that there are spies in the area, and they are searching the villages.”

John drove on and prayed that they were not discovered. They passed a Bedouin family who waved at the passing vehicle. John and Ishmael waved back but didn't slow down or stop.

John noticed something and suddenly hit the brakes. “Wait a minute, Ishmael."

“What is it?” Ishmael asked.

"I see something we need to check out." John had already turned the vehicle around and was headed back towards the Bedouins. They pulled up to the tent, and John jumped out and ran over to a line that had been strung from one tent pole to another. It held a skirt that was very familiar.

"You want to buy?" a small girl asked in broken English. "Where did you get this?" John demanded.

The girl lowered her head and said, "No understanding."

Ishmael repeated the question in her language, and she told him, "We are in the desert."

Ishmael turned to John and wanted to know why he was asking about the skirt. "It is rude to ask questions this way. They will be insulted," he said.

"This is Ingrid's skirt. Look at the label. It was made in Belgium. I remember seeing her wear this."

The little girl was whispering something to her mother, who walked over and began talking to a man a few yards away tending the sheep.

The man approached Ishmael and spoke. "We found it in the desert many days ago," he said.

John noticed some other pieces of clothing on the line that belonged to Ingrid. "I don't believe you," he yelled and grabbed the man by the neck. "Tell me the truth. Where did you get this clothing?"

CHAPTER 26 - INGRID

A loud noise was coming from the courtyard outside Ingrid's cell. It sounded like something or someone was attempting to crash through the fence. She heard gunfire and an explosion. She was afraid to move.

She heard the footsteps of what sounded like two or three people coming down the hall. When they stopped in front of Ingrid's cell door, she was afraid to look up. She thought, "They're coming for me. They're going to kill me." She whispered softly, "Oh dear God, please not me. Not now. I will never get to see my mother and sister again. And John will never know what happened to me."

A tall, skinny guard opened the door with a grin on his face. "Come with us." He grabbed her arm and jerked her off the bunk.

"Where are we going?" Ingrid asked. He didn't reply.

As they led her down the hall, Ingrid saw several other prisoners, mostly young Israeli men and women. Ingrid noticed a beautiful young girl with long black hair in one of the cells they passed. Ingrid could hear her softly crying.

They walked outside, and Ingrid was blinded by the bright sunlight. It was the first time she had been in the sun in several weeks. She stumbled and one of the guards grabbed her arm. "In the car," he said as they shoved her into the backseat and climbed on each side of her. The car sped away.

"At least they didn't shoot me," Ingrid thinks to herself. But where are they taking me?

They drove to a nearby village and pulled the

car into a garage in a large concrete building. It was hot inside, and Ingrid noticed all the windows were boarded up. The men dragged Ingrid out of the car and stood her against a wall. "This is the end," she thought. "They're going to shoot me."

Suddenly, one of the guards grabbed her hair and held a gun to her head. The other guard opened the trunk and pulled out a video camera. "You will say that we treat you well," they instructed. "You will say that if they release the five Hamas members captured last week, we will let you live. If you don't say that, you will die."

Ingrid hesitated, and the tall guard punched her in the stomach. She doubled over in pain and could hardly breathe.

"You will say it now," he insisted.

As soon as Ingrid could stand up, she repeated what she had been told to say. After they had turned off the camera, they took her to a small room off to the side that was worse than her jail cell and locked her in. There were no windows and no toilet, only a small cot pushed against the wall with a single light bulb mounted to the ceiling. Ingrid noticed what appeared to be blood stains on the floor and felt sure she was not the first prisoner held in the room.

She lay down on the cot and closed her eyes. She silently prayed that somehow God would deliver her from the hands of these cruel people. "Please dear God, let someone find me. Please let me have another chance to live in freedom. Please don't let my mother see that video." she whispered.

Several hours passed before Ingrid heard a key

rattling in the lock. A different man walked in and grabbed her arm and pulled her to her feet. “You must say again. You must convince them that we will kill you,” he whispered in her ear as he gripped her arm more tightly. He was close to her face and she could smell his sour breath. She tried to loosen her arm from his grip, but he was too strong. The many months in prison had weakened her muscles.

One of the men with a short beard picked up the video camera and began taping. The man holding Ingrid's arm pulled out a pistol and held it to her right temple. Ingrid noticed that the hammer was back on the automatic weapon, so she didn’t move. Slowly she repeated what she had been told to say. With tears rolling down her cheeks, she looked into the camera and said, “Please help me. I only have twenty-four hours to live.” She told the camera that she was a Fox News reporter. She felt certain that no one who knew her would recognize her now. She had lost a great deal of weight and was only almost skin and bones.

When the camera was turned off, Ingrid was shoved back into the room. The short man walked away, but the other one stood over her for a few minutes. She was afraid he might rape her. She whispered a prayer, and he finally walked away with a disgusted look on his face. “Thank you, God,” she whispered.

CHAPTER 27 – JOHN and ISHMAEL

John and his guide drove through the hot, steamy desert in silence for several hours. Ishmael was studying his map and John was driving and praying.

They arrived in a small, dirty village many miles from the Syrian border. The walls were dingy from years of sand blowing against them. Most of the buildings had no windows. Several young men were sitting against the walls or on crude wooden benches talking with each other. They all stared at the vehicle as John drove slowly past them. The streets had several carts that were pulled by vendors selling everything from Cokes to cigarettes. A few of them were selling food that they had prepared. However, John had learned years before never to eat food sold by a street vendor in a foreign country. One time when he bought some chicken from a street vendor's cart in Indonesia, he had learned that painful and valuable lesson.

They finally found a building that looked like a hotel. They pulled to the sidewalk, and Ishmael got out and went inside to check on rooms. He came back with a smile and said they could rest here for a few hours. Slowly John dragged himself from the Land Rover and grabbed his luggage.

Inside there was a small reception area with a wooden desk and a middle-aged man sitting behind it. He gave them a nod of his head as the men passed headed towards the wooden stairs off to the side. Each step required more effort from John – his feet hurt, his back hurt, and most of all, his heart hurt. John dropped his luggage beside the door as he entered and went to bed, and soon fell asleep.

Sometime later, Ishmael pounded on his door. "Mr. John, Mr. John. You must wake up."

John dragged himself to the door, twisted the small lock, and let him in. "What's up," John mumbled.

"Sit down," he ordered. "I have news." He started telling John that in the lobby there was a small TV that picked up the Arab television network. Ishmael talked excitedly, "Ingrid was on TV with a terrorist holding a gun to her head! She said that they will kill her unless Israel releases five Hamas terrorists. They have given her only twenty-four more hours to live!" he continued. "We must hurry!" he said as he headed for the door. "I will get the Land Rover. You get dressed."

Within fifteen minutes they were rolling out of the small village headed for Syria. As they drove, John prayed that somehow God would help them find a way to rescue her before it was too late.

They discussed how they might get into Syria without being detained. "It will not be easy," said Ishmael. "But maybe I know a way."

"I sure hope so," said John.

They drove a couple of hours, and eventually Ishmael drove behind a small hut in a village. "We need to get a few things out of the back," he suggested and moved quickly to open the tailgate and pull out a few necessities.

They walked through a small alley strewn with debris and came to a side entrance of a small hut. Ishmael unlocked the door and entered without turning on any lights. John stepped inside and stopped while his eyes adjusted to the darkness. Ishmael closed the door. “Follow me,” he said.

John stepped through the doorway and discovered a narrow set of wooden steps. They descended the steps in the dark, and Ishmael turned on a flashlight.

“We should be safe here for a while. It will be easier to cross the border after dark, when the guards are not as thorough in their interrogations,” he said as he sat down on the small case he had been carrying. “This is the house of my uncle. He died last year, and no one lives here now. There are no windows down here, so no one will know we are here.”

He then unfolded two small cots and set them up on each side of the room. “You will rest there," he pointed to the one near the stairs.”

John walked over and sat his briefcase on the floor at the head of the bed and lay down. He was asleep in a few short minutes.

A little later, Ishmael said, “I will return in twenty minutes,” and headed up the stairs.

John found a small washstand with a pitcher of water and splashed a little on his face. When Ishmael returned, he had a loaf of bread, some fruit, and two bottles of water. He offered half to John. As soon as they finished eating, they headed off.

When they stepped outside, it was dark. Within minutes, they were winding back through the narrow streets to the main road toward Syria.

“We will go to someone I know where we can get fake passports. You will never get in with your American papers,” he stated. “I learned in the village this morning that the war in Afghanistan drags on.”

When they were still many miles away from the

border, Ishmael suddenly swerved off the main road and took a narrow trail. He slipped the vehicle into four-wheel drive since they were traveling over extremely rough terrain. “We must be very careful here," he points out. "There are land mines near the border, and this is the only safe trail that I know of.”

After a few hours of slow travel, they saw another small village in the distance. The sun was hot and the glare on the windshield made it difficult to follow the trail. Finally, they wound their way into the village and stopped at a small cafe. They got out and walked inside. There were several men in a corner sitting around a table eating hummus and flatbread. They looked up and briefly examined John and Ishmael, then went back to eating.

Ishmael went to the owner and whispered something in his ear. The owner said, “Follow me.” They followed him into a small room. A small table off to the side contained a laptop computer, printer, and camera. He motioned for them to sit and proceeded to take their pictures. Within a few minutes, he had produced a very authentic looking Syrian passport for each of them. They paid him and left through the back door.

They walked through a narrow alley filled with old barrels and debris. As they rounded the corner, they were met by two men with rifles pointed at them.

"Who are you?” they demanded in English. Ishmael spoke to them in their native language. They lowered their guns and walked away.

“What did you say to them?” John asked.

“I told them that we were with Hamas and that they should let us pass.” John smiled as they got into the Land Rover and drove toward the Syrian border.

When they arrived at the border, Ishmael talked

with the guards before showing their passports. The guards glanced at the passports and at John and then waved them on. John let out a huge sigh, amazed that it had gone so smoothly. He realized, however, that Ishmael had family in Syria, and John guessed he had told them they were going to visit family.

They drove for several hours and came to a remote hillside. Ishmael drove up the side of the hill and stopped just below the top. He looked at John and indicated that he should wait in the vehicle. He slipped out the driver's side door, closed it gently, and crawled up to the crest of the hill. John saw him scan the countryside with his binoculars for a long time.

When he started back down the hill in a slow, backward crawl, John noticed that suddenly, he stopped. Not moving a muscle, he looked like a man paralyzed. John saw a look of terror on his face, so he opened his door and asked Ishmael what was wrong. Ishmael indicated that John should back the vehicle down the hill. Then he whispered, "Goodbye."

“What's wrong?" John asked after backing the Land Rover a couple of hundred feet and hurrying back up the trail towards Ishmael.

“I am on a landmine," he whispered. "When I move again, I will be killed, you must go on alone my friend, I am sorry I cannot continue with you.” As he said this, he moved, and the mine exploded. John watched in horror as his guide who had become his friend was blown to pieces.

“What do I do now?” he cried out loud. “Here I am in the middle of one of the most violent nations in the world. I don’t speak the language. I don’t have a clue where I am, or where to go and I don’t know where to look for Ingrid.”

He sat in the Land Rover for a long time before he

thought about the fact that someone might have heard the explosion and was searching for the location. He backed the vehicle slowly down the hill to the dirt trail and started driving. He drove until it was almost dark then pulled behind some small bushes and stopped. He laid his head on the headrest, lowered the seat, and eventually fell asleep.

CHAPTER 28 - INGRID

At the female voice coming from the TV, Joel Black turned suddenly in his chair to look at the screen. "That's Ingrid!" he exclaimed. "Dear God! She's alive!" he said as he swung around, jumped out of his chair, and headed out the door and down the hall.

He rushed into the office of the CEO and said, "Ingrid is still alive! We just showed a segment from the Arab network, and the hostage the terrorists are holding is Ingrid. She's alive but in terrible danger. We must do something right away."

"OK, Joel. Calm down. Let's figure out our options here." Fred Brunner, the CEO, picked up his phone and started dialing. After a brief but thorough discussion with his senior staff, Fred called the White House and was quickly dispatched to the President's office. The President agreed to have his chief of staff see what he could find out.

Two hours later, the President called saying that they'd had a discussion with the Israeli government who had agreed to exchange five low-level Hamas leaders in exchange for Ingrid. The exchange would take place at 6:00 am near the Syrian border.

Fred instructed Joel to book a flight to Israel immediately. There was a direct flight to Tel Aviv that would leave in four hours. Fortunately, as an experienced journalist, Joel always kept a bag packed in his office. He called his wife, picked up his bag, stopped by the bank to exchange currency, and headed to the airport.

As he waited for the boarding call for his flight, he called Fox human resources department and got the phone number for Ingrid's mother. He placed a call to her telling her that he knew Ingrid was alive and that Fox was doing everything possible to get her home safe. After the conversation, he sat back thinking and praying for a smooth swap and for Ingrid's safety.

Joel's flight was called, and he took his seat. He started thinking about what may need to be accomplished to get Ingrid to safety. He made a list of contacts. At the top of the list was the name of a doctor he knew who worked at Israel's best hospital. He knew from Ingrid's appearance on the videotape that she needed immediate medical attention.

After a very long flight, the plane landed in Tel Aviv. Joel's office had arranged a limo to take him to Jerusalem. After a 45-minute ride, he checked into a hotel to await a message from the prime minister. Joel tried not to focus too heavily on Ingrid's condition, but it was hard not thinking about what must have happened to her during the many months of her confinement.

Another hour passed before his cell phone rang. "Hello, Joel Black here" he answered. "Mister Black, we have her," the voice on the other end said after identifying themselves.

"Take her to the hospital right away. I have arranged for a doctor to take care of her. I will meet you there," Joel said as he rushed out the door.

After a short cab ride, Joel walked into the hospital and was immediately escorted by the security guard to the examining room where Ingrid was located. Tears formed in his eyes as he looked at her frail frame. There were circles around her eyes and her skin was drawn and pale. It was obvious that she had nearly starved. He laid his hand on hers and gently squeezed. "Thank God you're alive," he whispered.

Ingrid stirred and opened her eyes. She gave him a faint smile and closed her eyes. “Rest, Ingrid. You're safe now,” Joel whispered. He sat in the chair and closed his eyes. Tired from his long journey and relieved over Ingrid's release, he was soon asleep also.

The sun was shining brightly into the room when Joel woke up. Ingrid, with several IVs hooked to her arms, was still sleeping.

When Dr. Rosenbaum walked in, Joel was anxious to hear his report.

“She is in very bad condition. Her blood work reveals that most of her body chemicals are out of balance. She is dehydrated, and she has a great deal of bruising on her body. She was probably recently tortured. My guess is that she was tied and beaten before she was released. However, I believe that in time she will mend and be OK. We will keep her here for several days and treat her.”

“Thanks, doctor. I know you will take good care of her. I am so glad you were here to help her,” Joel said.

“You are welcome, old friend. And how have you been? It has been a long time since you were here in a similar condition.”

“I healed well, thanks to you, and I'm doing fine. But I am confined to an office now. It's difficult for me to travel as I once did, with this limp and other damage caused by the injuries,” Joel responded.

“You were one of the lucky ones to have survived the torture Hamas delivered to you ten years ago,” Dr. Rosenbaum replied. “You were very lucky, my friend.”

Joel looked down. “Yes. I know. God was good to me to have allowed me to be found and brought here to you.”

“I must go now and check on my other patients.

We will talk more later," the doctor said as he exited the room.

As soon as the doctor left the room, Joel called Ingrid's mother to fill her in on Ingrid's condition. She had, of course, been ecstatic over Ingrid's release and was thankful that she was getting medical care. "Thank you, Mr. Black," she muttered in a shaky voice.

Joel left the hospital and went back to the hotel to shower and find somewhere to have lunch. After lunch, he went back to the hospital to be with Ingrid. As he entered her room, he gently touched her hand. Her eyes opened slightly. She tried to speak but her voice was so weak he had a hard time hearing her. Joel leaned closer to her to catch what she was saying. "Call John Martin," she whispered.

"Who is he, and how do I find him?" Joel asked. She whispered a phone number. Joel immediately wrote it down and left the room to dial the number.

"Hello, John Martin's office," the female voice on the other end answered.

"Hello, my name is Joel Black with Fox News. I am calling from Israel for Mr. Martin." After a lengthy discussion with John's assistant, Joel realized that John was someone very special to Ingrid and that he was somewhere in Jordan searching for her. Joel also learned that John had not been heard from in over a week.

When he returned to Ingrid's room, Joel was unsure what he should tell her, so he simply whispered, "His secretary is trying to get word to him that you are here." A faint smile crossed her lips, and she was once again asleep. In her sleep, she whispered "I love you, John. I love you."

Joel stepped out of Ingrid's room again and

placed another call to Ingrid's mother. After reassuring her that Ingrid was resting comfortably, he asked, "What can you tell me about John Martin?" She filled Joel in on their relationship and what she knew about John's search for Ingrid. Joel hung up with some sadness. He thought about the kind of person John must be that he would leave everything and search for months for this woman. "Where could he be now?" he wondered. Joel could not help but fear the worst since no one knew where John was, and no one had been able to reach him for over a week.

As the days went by, Ingrid grew stronger. Joel finally told her what he knew about John and the fact that no one had heard from him in some time. Tears slid down her cheeks as she listened. "Oh John, where are you?" she whispered.

After a week, Ingrid was strong enough to leave the hospital. After a great deal of pressure by Joel, Ingrid agreed to fly to New York with him for additional medical tests. After a week in New York, she was released to return home.

"Ingrid, why don't you take a few weeks to rest? Go visit your mother," Joel suggested. "We will continue to search for John. If we learn anything, we will call you immediately."

Ingrid boarded a plane and headed home to stay with her mother in Luxembourg. When she arrived in Brussels, her mother and sister were waiting for her. On the drive to Kettelbruck, they filled her in on what they knew about John and his search for her. As she lay in bed that night, she prayed like she had never prayed before, asking God to keep John safe and bring him home to her.

CHAPTER 29 - JOHN

John was awakened by a distant noise that sounded like small children playing. He rubbed his eyes and looked through the windshield. There were two small Bedouin boys chasing some goats. They laughed as they herded the goats off in the direction of what must be their camp.

John started the Land Rover and drove down the road in the direction the boys had gone. He tried to stay far enough behind them that he would not startle them. As he reached the top of a hill, he saw their camp nestled in a small valley. He got out of the vehicle and slowly approached a man who was coming out of one of the tents toward the dirt road where John had stopped.

The Bedouin spoke no English, so communication was difficult. After lots of hand motions by both, John was able to get him to understand. The man directed John to the nearest road which was nothing more than a trail that was rocky and very rough. After a few miles, John found a paved road. Then the big decision was which direction he should take. After a brief hesitation, he headed west toward the late afternoon sun.

John drove for about an hour before he met any other vehicles. The few road signs he saw made little sense to him since he could not read them. He assumed that he was going in the direction of the Israeli border, but he wasn't certain. There had been so much violence in Syria in recent months as insurgents attempted to remove the country's leader from power. Many had died and John realized that this was not a place to be lost in. His daily prayers were for Ingrid's safety and their eventual reuniting.

As the sun was sinking behind the horizon, John saw what he thought was a border crossing ahead. He quickly pulled off the highway and tried to decide what to do. If he approached with his fake Syrian passport, he might be able to get through, but without Ishmael's charm and persuasion, John wasn't sure he could pull it off.

He finally decided to wait until after dark and attempt to slip across the border. If he could make it to the Israeli side and talk to their border guards, he might have a better chance of getting to Jerusalem. All the time, in the back of his mind, he feared that Ingrid may have been killed since the twenty-four-hour period had passed that the terrorists had imposed. He tried to avoid thinking that way and focus on his current predicament. Maybe I should just take my chances and run across the border, he thought. He gathered the few essential belongings he thought he might need, opened the door, and slipped to the ground.

He made his way through the underbrush and low shrubs as he inched his way to the border. He expected a barbed wire barricade, but he saw none. Then it occurred to him that there might be landmines buried in the sand. He had no idea how to find a land mine, so he prayed and continued to inch forward in the sand.

Inch by inch he continued until he thought he was across the border. He slowly lifted his head to try to see where the guard shack was located when he heard a bullet whizz by his head and land a few feet away in the sand. He jumped up and started to run when suddenly he felt a burning in his side. He had been shot. He heard a shout. As he lay motionless on the ground, he thought he might be dying. A few minutes later, he felt someone dragging him and realized that he had crossed the border. He was being half dragged and half pulled by Israeli soldiers toward their building. Once inside, they placed him on a wooden bench and began to examine him.

John tried to speak but was unable to say anything. The Israelis, after some discussion and a search of his belongings, saw his American passport and decided to take him to a hospital. They put a bandage over his wound and transported him in the back of a truck to a hospital. A few minutes into the trip, John passed out.

Three days later, John regained consciousness. Still dazed, he gazed around the room and tried to remember what had happened and where he was. A nurse entered the room to check on him and saw that he was awake. He attempted to talk but was so weak that the words seemed to evaporate before leaving his lips. “Rest, sir,” the nurse whispered. “You lost a lot of blood, and you need to rest. Don’t try to talk,” she said as she left the room.

Later that evening, a doctor walked in and sat in a chair beside John. “Young man,” he started. "You lost a lot of blood from the two gunshot wounds you received crossing the border. We believe that you will recover, but it will not happen overnight. We are attempting to notify your family; however, we have left several messages, but no one has called us back.” He continued, “We are waiting for a call. Does anyone live there with you?”

John shook his head from side to side.

“I see,” the doctor said. “Is there anyone else we should try to call?” the doctor asked. John tried to whisper a phone number, but it was difficult for the doctor to hear him. Finally, the doctor thought he had the number and said, “OK, we will try this number.”

Halfway around the world a phone rang. After three rings, John’s assistant answered the phone. “John Martin’s office,” she said. The doctor quickly explained to her that John was alive and in a hospital in Jerusalem and was expected to recover completely. She thanked the doctor and immediately called Joel Black with the news.

Joel was delighted to hear that John was alive and safe. He immediately called Ingrid in Luxembourg. “Ingrid,” he began, “you might want to sit down. I have some news for you.”

Time seemed to stand still while Ingrid waited for Joel to continue. “John is alive, and he is in a hospital in Jerusalem. He was shot and is in serious condition. However, the doctor thinks that given adequate time, he will make a complete recovery.”

“Thanks so much for calling me, Joel,” Ingrid said. She snapped the cell phone closed as the dam had just burst and tears started flowing down her cheeks. She felt a tremendous sense of relief and worry at the same moment. Ingrid's mother walked into the room and asked, “What's wrong, my dear girl?” Ingrid tried to talk but the words stuck in her throat. Her mother wrapped her arms around her and reassured her. After Ingrid had calmed, she told her about Joel's call.

“I must go to Jerusalem,” she said and picked up her cell phone again to call the airline. There was a flight leaving at 9:30 that night to Tel Aviv. Ingrid booked a seat and immediately started to pack. As she left, she hugged her mother and told her she would call when she had more news. As she drove away, Ingrid prayed, “God, please heal John. I know you can heal him,” she said out loud as she headed out of town past the statue of General George Armstrong Patton.

After Ingrid boarded the plane and found her seat, she immediately closed her eyes in prayer. A few hours later, she awoke realizing that she had fallen asleep. She felt hopeful and could hardly wait to see John.

When the plane landed, she grabbed her bag, caught a cab, and headed for Jerusalem. In less than an hour, the cab dropped her in front of David Ben Gurion Hospital. She quickly walked inside and headed for the elevator and the room number that Joel had given her. Her heart was pounding as she approached the door to John's room. Her hands were wet with perspiration when she reached to turn the knob. She had tried during the cab ride to mentally prepare herself for what she might find when she saw him but was shocked by what she saw.

As light coming through the door touched the face of the man in the bed, Ingrid saw someone who resembled John, but he did not look like the John she remembered. He had lost a lot of weight. His head was shaved because a bullet had grazed his skull. He had IV lines in both arms and a monitor attached to his chest. His hands were black and blue, his lips were pale, and his skin was dry and cracked. She felt herself swaying but caught herself and shook off the feeling. She reminded herself that she must be strong, and she slowly approached the bed. She sat in the chair beside his bed and gently touched his hand. Nothing happened. She continued to hold his hand and silently pray for him.

“He went through all this for me Lord,” she

prayed. "I know he could have died but I also know that you saved him. I have never known this kind of love for another person. This man is the love of my life. Please heal him," she prayed.

Hours later, John opened his eyes and saw what he thought must be an angel. “Oh God,” he prayed, “have I died and gone to heaven and now see an angel?” Then suddenly he realized what he saw was for real – he was looking at Ingrid.

“Ingrid?” he whispered. “Ingrid?” he whispered again.

She opened her eyes and leaned towards him “Oh, John.

You're awake,” she said.

“Are we in heaven?” he asked.

“No," she said with a huge smile. "At least not God's heaven, not yet," she continued as tears rolled down her cheeks. "We are both alive, and we are going to be together now and forever,” she said. They held hands for hours.

Over the next few weeks, they were together day and night as they shared their stories and their dreams of a future together with each other. Day by day, they both healed and grew stronger. They prayed together daily, thanking God for bringing them together and for bringing them through the last few months of horror.

On a bright, sunny morning in Jerusalem, Ingrid and John walked out of the hospital together. They were headed for the airport. They held onto each other as they headed for Tel Aviv and the flight to Colorado. They knew that this was the beginning of the rest of their lives together.

EPILOGUE

One year later, Ingrid and John were walking on the beach by the Baltic Sea. They had purchased a small home by the sea and spent most of their summers there. They lived in Colorado in John's cabin in the Rocky Mountains during the winter. They still had the paintings they had bought together long ago in Bruges that were hanging side by side in the cabin. They had each written a book about their experiences and about their search for love – a love that had been lost and then found.

Their favorite time of day along the Baltic was the late afternoon. They sat in their chairs and held hands as the sun set over the sea. They never forgot to thank God for allowing them to have a life together. Ingrid often looked at John as they held hands and reminded him that this was paradise. “,” she would say with a soft voice and a sweet smile.

www.ingramcontent.com/pod-product-compliance
Lightning Source LLC
Chambersburg PA
CBHW070543310726
48982CB00010B/1463/J

* 9 7 8 1 7 3 4 7 4 8 1 2 3 *